D0815691

"Olsson explores the hard-won wisdom that can come through grief. . . . Olsson's dense, magisterial prose pulls the reader in immediately, and Adam's profound sadness is perfectly handled. . . . It's palpable, but never saccharine or overbearing as the narrative builds toward its unexpected conclusion."

—*Publishers Weekly*

Praise for *Astrid & Veronika*

"Linda Olsson's novel casts the themes of secrecy, passion, and loss in the shape of a double helix, intertwining the stories of two women. . . . Natural and vivid, utterly convincing . . . simply so beguiling."

—*The New York Times Book Review*

"Linda Olsson evokes, with great precision and beauty, the landscape of a friendship. . . . *Astrid & Veronika* is penetrating and beautifully written, and it affirms the power of narrative to transform."

—Kim Edwards, author of *The Memory Keeper's Daughter*

"Beautiful and deeply affecting. A dreamlike evocation of the power of friendship." —Mary McGarry Morris, author of *The Lost Mother* and *Songs in Ordinary Time*

"Readers of Anne Tyler and Jodi Picoult will appreciate the lyrical prose and expert rendering of the themes of heartbreak and loss." —*Booklist*

"What separates this debut from the rest of the crowd is Olsson's deft writing. Her descriptions are beautiful, capable of both painting the scene and creating a mood. . . . Booksellers from around the country as well as locally have raved about *Astrid & Veronika*. It's easy to understand why." —*Portland Tribune*

"Has the hallmarks of an Ingmar Bergman film: a leisurely pace, a chilly Scandinavian setting leavened by rich observations of nature, and characters whose prim, polite facades eventually disappear, exposing years of anger and hurt." —*Kirkus Reviews*

PENGUIN BOOKS

THE MEMORY OF LOVE

© CAROLINE ANDERSSON

Linda Olsson was born in Stockholm, Sweden, in 1948. She graduated from the University of Stockholm with a law degree and worked in law and finance until she left Sweden in 1986. What was intended as a three-year posting to Kenya then became a tour of the world with stops in Singapore, the United Kingdom, and Japan, until she settled in New Zealand with her family in 1990. In 1993 she completed a bachelor of arts in English and German literature at Victoria University of Wellington. In 2003 she won the *Sunday Star-Times* Short Story Competition. Olsson's first novel, *Astrid & Veronika*, became an international success, selling hundreds of thousands of copies in Scandinavia, Europe, and the United States. It was followed by the heartbreaking and moving *Sonata for Miriam*. Olsson divides her time between Auckland, New Zealand, and Stockholm, Sweden.

The
Memory
of Love

Linda Olsson

PENGUIN BOOKS

PENGUIN BOOKS

Published by the Penguin Group
Penguin Group (USA) Inc., 375 Hudson Street, New York, New York 10014, U.S.A.
Penguin Group (Canada), 90 Eglinton Avenue East, Suite 700, Toronto,
Ontario M4P 2Y3, Canada (a division of Pearson Penguin Canada Inc.)
Penguin Books Ltd, 80 Strand, London WC2R 0RL, England
Penguin Ireland, 25 St Stephen's Green, Dublin 2, Ireland (a division of Penguin Books Ltd)
Penguin Group (Australia), 707 Collins Street, Melbourne, Victoria 3008, Australia
(a division of Pearson Australia Group Pty Ltd)
Penguin Books India Pvt Ltd, 11 Community Centre, Panchsheel Park, New Delhi–110 017, India
Penguin Group (NZ), 67 Apollo Drive, Rosedale, Auckland 0632,
New Zealand (a division of Pearson New Zealand Ltd)
Penguin Books (South Africa), Rosebank Office Park, 181 Jan Smuts Avenue,
Parktown North 2193, South Africa
Penguin China, B7 Jiaming Center, 27 East Third Ring Road North,
Chaoyang District, Beijing 100020, China

Penguin Books Ltd, Registered Offices:
80 Strand, London WC2R 0RL, England

First published in New Zealand as *The Kindness of Your Nature* by Penguin Group (NZ) 2011
Published in Penguin Books (USA) 2013

1   3   5   7   9   10   8   6   4   2

PUBLISHER'S NOTE
This is a work of fiction. Names, characters, places, and incidents either are the product
of the author's imagination or are used fictitiously, and any resemblance to actual persons,
living or dead, businesses, companies, events, or locales is entirely coincidental.

ISBN 978-0-14-312243-2
CIP data available

Printed in the United States of America
Designed by Anna Egan-Reid
Chapter openers designed by Sara Bellamy

For my mother

The pact that we made was the ordinary pact
of men & women in those days

I don't know who we thought we were
that our personalities
could resist the failures of the race

Lucky or unlucky, we didn't know
the race had failures of that order
and that we were going to share them

Like everybody else, we thought of ourselves as special

Your body is as vivid to me
as it ever was: even more

since my feeling for it is clearer:
I know what it could and could not do

it is no longer
the body of a god
or anything with power over my life

Next year it would have been 20 years
and you are wastefully dead
who might have made the leap
we talked, too late, of making

which I live now
not as a leap
but a succession of brief, amazing movements

each one making possible the next

'From a Survivor' by Adrienne Rich

The Memory *of* Love

1.

It was Thursday and I was making soup. By now it was an established routine. Greek fish soup this week. I was boiling the vegetables, and steam covered the window above the sink. The kitchen faced the beach with an unobstructed view of the endless sea, which at that moment was just a grey blur behind the film of condensation. I had cleaned the fish, three small snapper, and I was making the avgolemono, the lemon and egg sauce. The lemons were scruffy to look at, but as I cut them the fragrance filled the kitchen. The lemons from the tree behind the house seemed to have more taste and a more intense smell than any I had ever come across anywhere else. I whipped the egg whites, folded the yolks into them and then I added the lemon juice. I chopped the parsley, and it was all prepared. All that remained was to allow the vegetables to boil till they had softened, add the fish, and then at the last minute stir in the avgolemono and parsley. I had time to go and sit on the doorstep for a moment. I kept a hammock and a few rattan chairs on the deck, but I seldom used them. I preferred the doorstep.

'Marianne,' I said to myself. 'Marianne.'

Lately, I had felt the need to taste the name. To listen to it. Retrieve it, perhaps. It was still a strange experience – I didn't quite own it yet. Or perhaps it was mine but in another, distant time, locked inside another room. I had made it a habit to try it several times every day. I couldn't quite remember when I began, but it had been some time. I wondered how it would sound to others: a middle-aged woman sitting on the doorstep of her house repeating her own name. But there was nobody around. Just Kasper, my ginger cat; his slowly blinking green eyes looked as if they had seen everything, accepted everything. He sat beside me, close, but not too close, still in his own sphere. As we both liked it, I think. Beside each other, but separate. As always, he sat calm and patient while I did my strange exercises. Or whatever one might have called them.

'Marianne,' I repeated. It was odd to feel how my body responded to the sound. After all these years.

It felt hot. The colour was red, and the name burned on my tongue before it lifted off my lips like a flame.

Marion, on the other hand, fell from my lips light blue, almost grey. Pale and cool. And it dissolved instantly.

Marion.

Marianne.

I stood and walked across the deck and down the stairs onto the sand. The dry grass on the dunes rustled in the light wind. I turned and looked at my house for a moment. The small weatherboard structure had become an integral part of my own physical self and I rarely consciously regarded it. I took a few steps back and looked at it where it sat on the sand in front of me. There was sand inside and out. It no longer bothered me and I had long given up all efforts at keeping it off the floors. I spent most of my time outside and I liked the idea that the distinction between inside and outside had become increasingly blurred. It was as if the house and all it contained was slowly dissolving and would eventually become one with the sand it sat on. These days I walked barefoot across the threshold without wiping the sand off my feet. It had taken me a long time to reach this state.

I knew that most people would say the house needed paint. But I liked it as it was, polished by the wind and the salt from the sea. It had become a soft grey, in some lights almost silvery, and the boards were smooth and soft to the touch.

'Absolute beachfront' was what it had said in the brochure. It was a selling point then. Not so any more, I suspected. At least not on this coast with soft and low dunes, only just rising over the surface of the sea. The view had remained the same, of course. Impossible to ignore, even after all these years. The never-ending sea, subtly changing colour and character from one moment to the next. Never the same, yet always the same. Even before any mention of the greenhouse effect and melting polar ice, the dunes had provided a shifting, uncertain base for a house. October storms often swallowed large chunks of sand and washed them out to sea. I didn't mind the sense of uncertainty. The precariousness of my existence. That lingering subconscious awareness of the slowly rising tide that would one day prise my house off the ground and sweep it out to sea. Or the giant wave that would lift it up in one quick rolling thunder. I preferred that scenario. And I would concede. I had convinced myself that I was ready.

But till that day I was going to stay put. I walked along the beach every morning. When I had first returned to make my home in this place I had started my walks as something to give my existence some shape and form. Or perhaps as something to cling to. But the tentative, dutiful walks had eventually become purposeful routine, in a way also part of my work. If you could call it that. It was during my morning walks that I gathered my material. Driftwood. Stones and shells. Nuts and seeds. Feathers and bones. All polished by the sea and soft in my hands, each piece in its own way. There had been no particular purpose behind the gathering at first. My eyes would absent-mindedly set on a piece of wood rolling in the foam at the edge of the withdrawing sea and I would bend down and pick it up. Keep it in my hand while I walked on. Or it could be a stone, always more colourful where it lay on the wet sand than dry in my hand. But soft, always. Soothing. Later I had begun to carry a basket, and over time the gathering had become purposeful. It had changed the nature of my walks of course. They were no longer walks, really, but expeditions. Hunts. They continued to occupy my time and my thoughts.

They called me 'the artist'. And they called me 'the doctor'. Or just 'her' or 'that foreign woman'. Making it clear that somehow I was not one of them. To them I had no name, just a designation. It was a kind community though. Non-judgemental, mostly. Perhaps they just didn't care. To some extent you could be what you wanted to be there. It was as if the place attracted a certain kind of people. Generous and open-minded. Not all, of course; there were others too. Like anywhere. Those who wanted to take rather than give. But on the whole they were decent people with a natural instinct to leave others to their own.

I had been thinking about that. This giving and taking. I had come to think that there were two kinds of people: those who produced and created, and those who lived off other people's labour. Not just in a material sense, and not just here, in my environment. To a lesser degree here than elsewhere, perhaps. No, generally, and everywhere. I wasn't even sure if one was better than the other. Perhaps both were needed to the same extent. But curiously it seemed to me that the latter – the takers – had somehow taken precedence. The reward seemed to have become higher for those who managed the result of the work of others than for the creators. Surely it hadn't always been so. I wondered when the balance had shifted and whether it would flow back again.

There I was, with my feet in the sand, foolishly trying to pretend that I was outside, or perhaps even above it all. That the world could not reach me or impact on my life. But there was no escaping the reality of the rest of the world. I was part of it by my sheer physical presence. This remote place where I existed was connected to the rest of the world in ways that I could not influence. I could ignore the world as much as I liked, but it would still be there and it would continue to affect me and my environment regardless of what I thought or did.

Behind the house was my small garden. Too elaborate a term perhaps for the small sandy patch where I grew tomatoes, lettuces, onions and herbs. And where my lemon tree lived, thwarted by the constant wind but still yielding its scrawny fruit generously. It must have been very old, older than the house. Older than me, probably. Its short knobbly trunk was wide at the base and carried scars where branches had been trimmed off. There was a grapefruit tree and a feijoa beside it, but they were new companions to the lemon tree. In the early days I had considered planting potatoes and kumara and becoming more self-sufficient. But the idea of being restricted by the demands of a proper garden hadn't appealed to me. As it was, I could leave it for weeks and little happened. The tomatoes needed watering of course, but their resilience had surprised me when I had had to leave them unattended for several days.

Apart from my garden and my cat I had very little company. I met Sophie every now and then, but not very often any more. The whole idea with our shared surgery had always been that the one of us who was not on duty should be genuinely free. She was much younger than I and she had three young children. We had shared our surgery for several years and it had worked well. I had enjoyed my work, and perhaps the social side of it, the contact with my patients, had been a replacement for the private life I largely lacked. But then there had come a day when I had decided to retire. Spend more time on my creative work. We had changed our arrangement and I served as a locum from time to time. It seemed to be less and less frequently. My life became lonelier in a way, but also richer. I had very little in the way of human intercourse but I enjoyed the sense of freedom. I had arranged my life as it pleased me and it had felt like a state of being I would enjoy until the end of my life. But it hadn't quite worked out like that.

My nearest neighbour was a farmer up the hill on the other side of the road. George Brendel. I didn't know much about him but I had always been aware that, like me, he was not a local. He spoke with a slight accent that was evident only occasionally. He owned a substantial piece of land but he kept no other animals than a flock of sheep. Like George and me, they stood out too – they were not quite right in this environment. Firstly, sheep did not really belong in this part of the country. And also, George's sheep were small and had black legs. I had only seen such sheep once before – in Gotland in the Baltic Sea. It was a mystery where George's flock came from. They grazed under his olive trees – another oddity, as nobody grew olives here. Like their owner, the sheep had slowly claimed their right to exist here, not as proper locals, but as a tolerated oddity.

George's shortcomings as a farmer seemed to have one main cause: he had money. I had no idea where this notion had come from, but it seemed to be a common assumption: George Brendel was an incompetent farmer because he had money. He had lived here much longer than I, and over the years he had come to earn a kind of respect, if not as a farmer, then as a person. He was active in the community and he was on the board of the local council.

I had been to his farm, but never inside his house. I didn't think he had a family, but I didn't really know much about his private life. He kept saying he admired my art and when he bought something, he paid for it in meat, olive oil or favours. Always too generously. I regarded it as charity. Perhaps it was something entirely different that I was not keen to analyse. As we had slowly got to know each other a little, he sometimes lingered on my doorstep when he came to visit, as if there were something he wanted to say. Oddly, it didn't worry me, but I didn't encourage it either. I had never asked him inside. There had been a time when I wouldn't have been able to accept his gifts. And certainly would not have allowed him to linger. But over time I had come gratefully to accept his offerings, material and otherwise. It happened that I caught his gaze occasionally and held on to it for the briefest moment. But there had been no obvious response. He had taken no initiative, no action. Just that uncertain lingering on my threshold.

There were a few other neighbours who occasionally would give me fish and sometimes a crayfish. Even oysters and scallops. I suspected they pitied me and didn't think I was quite equipped to manage on my own. They were probably right. For many years my house was just a place where I slept after work. And a monument to my relentless grief. Years that had become a blur. It was only since I had taken early retirement and begun to invest more time in my art that I had started to live here properly. But even after all these years I had not become one of them – someone who could rightly lay claim to this place. To them I was still a temporary visitor. Someone they needed to look after.

And it suited both parties.

2.

For some time I had been filled with a growing sense of urgency. It hadn't happened suddenly, more like a slow progression of steps so minute I had not taken notice. But one day I became aware of a feeling of restlessness. As if there were something I urgently needed to address. I felt a strong need to put aspects of my life in some sort of order. It didn't concern anybody else, but even though it was something I needed to do just for me, it did feel acutely important. Why, I couldn't quite understand. My life had been the same for years, and I didn't expect any dramatic changes. Nothing had happened to prompt this shift. This sense of urgency.

But something *had* changed. And it must have been me, because everything around me was the same. Perhaps it was all just a natural consequence of ageing, a growing awareness of the finiteness of my existence. And it was inexorable – an inevitable process that I could not escape. Not that I felt a need to. In fact I embraced it with something close to anticipation.

When I say nothing around me had changed, it is not quite the whole truth. There was the boy. Ika. He had entered my life, and I didn't know exactly what to make of his presence. How it would affect me. Had already affected me. I took it one week at a time. But I had to admit to myself I had begun to look forward to Thursdays.

The space where I lived had undergone a subtle change too. Perhaps the sense of unease had something to do with this. There seemed to be a change in my perception of myself and my place. Although I suspected it must be the result of a long process, it was only recently that I had come to realise what constituted the difference: suddenly I had a sense of a view. A perspective that I had previously lacked. For the first time in my life I began to see myself in some kind of context. And in a strange way I felt as if others saw me differently too. Not in a real sense – there were very few people in my life – it was more that I had become aware of the potential. It felt as if I had always lived in closed spaces before. Until now there had been no view – from the inside looking out, or the outside looking in. But something seemed to have abruptly ripped open. It surprised me that I didn't feel exposed. Instead, I was filled with an inexplicable sense of anticipation. As if this opening of doors and tearing away of layers was a positive thing. Perhaps I was hoping it would help me to put the events of my life in some kind of order, help me see it as a whole. It was difficult to understand why this suddenly felt so important, when in the past the ability to close the door behind each segment of my life had seemed vital to my survival.

I realised it could all prove a futile exercise. I was not at all sure there could be order in the life of any human being. Life is irrational and illogical, and we have to accept that, and try to arrange our lives around it. But perhaps we do need to try to understand our own history. See it as a coherent whole.

There is a timeline to our lives. One event leads to another. One act produces a result, which becomes the basis for our next action. Looking at it like this we give our lives a kind of causality. I am not sure if this is an illusion, but I can understand that it is helpful.

Now I wanted it for me.

There seemed to be so many storylines though. So many characters acting independently in the dramas that made up my life. And they all seemed to influence each other in ways that were impossible to fully grasp.

Then, as now, I knew that there is no absolute certainty about anything. I once believed that science offered certainty. That there were scientific rules that were immutable. This might have been why I loved science at school. And why I chose to study medicine. Once I believed that science offered a world with absolute truths. But the deeper I delved, the less absolute it appeared. There were inconstancies there too. New research made previous truths obsolete. And always, beyond every answer and every explanation, there was another unanswered question. It was like plotting my way through territories that gradually became familiar, but with a constant growing awareness of another unknown or unknowable reality beyond. Every answer was followed by a question mark. Every step took me further into the unknown. And the unknown grew, while what I knew seemed to shrink.

I had lived in this small desolate place for nearly fifteen years. By myself, mostly. I didn't mind. Absolutely not. It was a self-induced state. But the isolation aggravated the uncertainty, I think, and my life had taken on a slightly surreal quality. For some time I had found myself wishing for a way of corroborating events, memories. I had started to yearn for some kind of confirmation that my memories were still intact.

I had nurtured my important memories and been careful not to wear them down or alter them in any way. I had tried to keep them safe, but they were not kept in order. I knew absolutely where each one was, and what it contained, but it existed in a kind of vacuum, separate from the others. I can't explain why it felt like that. It was as if I carried them as an unsorted bundle, present only as a constant weight.

I had come to think that if I were able to take them out one by one and place them in the right sequence, then perhaps they would be easier to carry. The painful ones might become more bearable if I could see each one as belonging to what went before and what came after. I think I was hoping for some understanding. And forgiveness, perhaps. Not from others but from myself so that I could finally regard myself with a measure of compassion. Not love – I certainly didn't expect that. Not pity, I absolutely didn't want that. But empathy, perhaps. For the little girl that was me. For the young woman I had been. And for the middle-aged person I had now become.

I think I was hoping for the memories to merge, to become an understandable whole.

And ultimately make me whole.

3.

So, it was Thursday. I was hoping Ika would come. I could not be sure, but I was reasonably hopeful. He was getting older: it had been almost a year since we first met. I had estimated that he was about six years old then. He still had his baby teeth. We stumbled on each other down on the beach. Or rather I stumbled on him. And where else? It was on the beach that our lives were enacted, whether tragedies or comedies. I found him lying face down in the sand with his feet touching the edge of the surf. It wasn't as if he had been brought ashore on it. No, I could see his footprints in the sand and knew he had deliberately placed himself there. His arms were outstretched and his hands dug into the sand. He looked like a stranded starfish, but for a split second I had a vision of the slim little body being crucified. The sea kept lapping at his feet. He didn't move, though I was sure he had sensed my presence.

Had anticipated it, even. There was something about him that made it clear he was certainly alive. He just wasn't capable of playing dead, if that was what he was doing. So, after the initial instinctive ocular check, I just stood and waited.

He can only hold this pose for so long, I thought.

I underestimated his perseverance. Yet he underestimated my patience even more. I was willing to wait for as long as it would take. So there he lay, and there I stood. I looked at the sky and asked if he was hungry. There was no response. The seagulls above were shrieking over the thunder of the waves. The tide was on its way out and each wave stopped a little further from the tips of his toes.

'Are you hungry?' I repeated to his immobile back. Still no answer. He didn't stir. The only sign of life was the rhythmic slight lift as his ribcage expanded and contracted with each breath.

We waited.

Eventually he slowly rolled over onto his back. His face was covered in sand and he kept his eyes closed. I stood looking down at him. I was sure I had never seen him before. Never at the clinic, which was odd. If he lived anywhere near, I probably should have. Then without a word he sprang to his feet and ran into the water. When he returned he was rinsed of the sand and his shorts and T-shirt clung to his body. He was painfully thin. I noted that he didn't seem to have many teeth, and those he had were baby teeth.

'Are you hungry?' I asked again.

He didn't look at me, said nothing, just dug his toes into the sand, half turned away from me. I turned and slowly began to walk away and I sensed that he was following. He made little detours to pick up a stone and throw it into the sea, to chase a bird. If I slowed down, he did too. When I stopped, so did he. When I started walking again he followed. Weaving up and down the dunes on either side.

It was a Thursday, the first one.

I could never be certain that he would come, but he came most Thursdays. He never explained his absences and I never asked. He never appeared on another day of the week.

He had become a source of information for me, though he didn't speak much. But for someone like me, even minute snippets of information about what went on outside my sphere were valuable. I often thought of myself as naïve. There had always been matters that other people seemed to consider normal and natural that I hadn't been able to understand. On the other hand, I had always felt there were matters that were familiar to me that would seem strange to others. Perhaps naïve was not the right word but I couldn't think of a better one.

He was also a source of profound wisdom. I worried that this capacity of his would pass. That he would grow out of it. I hoped not, but I could not be sure. As he was, he was an extraordinary human being. Non-judgemental. Curious. Funny sometimes, though I never knew if it was intentional. I couldn't believe he would ever lose those qualities, but I knew it was likely to happen. Time would rob him of them, or life would teach him how to suppress them. I cherished him. And I took one week at a time. One Thursday at a time. Inevitably he would change. And inevitably I would lose him one day.

I foolishly thought I could prepare myself for that.

It was a white day with little wind. As wintry as it gets here. It wasn't particularly cold, not by my standards. It was the light that made it clear it was winter, not the temperature. That peculiar west coast white winter light. It was as if the colour had been drained out of everything: the sky, the sea, the vegetation. Even me. I walked back and sat on the doorstep, let my eyes rest on the sea. The string of paua shells blew in the wind, occasionally rattling against the weatherboards. There was no sign of him but it was early yet. And the soup would take a while. I wasn't sure if he had a favourite, not even now after almost a year. He never commented on the food, but ate with the same constant diligence whatever I put in front of him. I made bread on Thursdays too. I used to make the dough in the morning before I set out, then bake it when I returned. It had become a weekly routine, just like the soup. There had been a time when I lived without routines, but I had come to depend on this one. Far too much, really.

Wintertime, I sometimes cooked yellow pea soup. Like my grandfather used to. It never came out quite like his as I remembered it, but I kept trying. In spite of my attempts at consistency, each time it somehow became a unique composition. Although I used the same ingredients: a hock of salted pork, onions, a bay leaf or two. A few peppercorns. Some marjoram, fresh when there was some in the garden, otherwise dried. Dried yellow peas that I soaked overnight. If I poured them into the cold water to cook with the pork they became soft and mushy; if I added them to the boiling water later, when the pork had cooked for a while, they came out firmer and the skins translucent. That's how I preferred them. But, as I said, it seemed to make no difference to my guest. I always used the only large pot I had and the leftovers lasted me several days. But no Thursday turned out the same, no soup the same as any other, and the pea soup never like my grandfather's. But that winter Thursday it was Greek fish soup.

One hot summer Thursday I had made a salad instead of soup, but it didn't go down well, I noticed, though he didn't say anything. So, soup it was. He seemed to like them all. Some were experiments, not always successful, but he never complained. And never complimented me either. Perhaps he was just too hungry to be discerning.

I thought his name was Mika, but ever since that first day when I had misheard him I had called him Ika and he didn't seem to mind. He told me it meant fish and I thought it suited him. Even before I saw his hands.

I had started when I first heard what he called me. Mama. It became his name for me. His very own. It wasn't that I was a sort of mother to him, I think. No, he told me it meant light. I wasn't sure if he meant light as in not heavy, or the opposite of darkness. I thought the former, but sometimes I liked to think he meant the latter. Whichever it was, I liked it.

'Why did you come here, Mama?' he asked one day, instinctively knowing that I had *come* here. From somewhere else.

'Well,' I said, 'it's a long story.' He looked at me. Or rather, in his usual fashion, he looked not quite *at* me, but at some point just beyond me. It seemed like a changeable point, with the sole purpose of being close to me but not quite *at* me. He didn't look as if he expected much in the way of reply, but his gaze remained on the same unspecified point.

'I first came here many years ago. On a holiday. And something happened to me here.' I hesitated.

'Was it happy or sad?' he asked.

'Sad,' I said. 'It was very sad.' I looked at him and added: 'At first it was happy though. As happy as anything can ever get.'

'It had to be happy first,' he said, and it sounded like a private reflection, not a piece of conversation.

I looked at him, but again could not catch his eyes.

'You're probably right. Perhaps nothing can be sad in itself.'

'So you left,' he said. It was a statement, not a question, but I nodded regardless. 'And then you came back.'

'I did. First, I came here for a holiday. Then I went back to my home far away. But I couldn't stop thinking about this place. I thought about it during the day, and I dreamt about it at night. Sad dreams. But also very beautiful. And this place became more and more important to me. One day I felt I had to come back here to live.'

'Are you always going to be here now?' He was fingering the edge of the table, running his hands over the wood. His nails were dirty and the skin across the knuckles bruised. He held the fingers closely together.

The impression was of someone trying to smooth the surface. I knew by then that crumbs made him uneasy, so I made it a habit to keep the table spotless.

I stood and collected our plates and walked over to the kitchen counter. I looked out the window. It was a sunny day with a light wind and the sea sparkled with blinding intensity.

'I think so,' I said with my back to him, 'but you can never be certain. Things change. You change, and everything around you changes. Things happen.' I returned to the table and sat down. 'But yes, I really do think I will stay here.'

He said nothing.

'How about you?' I asked. 'Will you always stay here?'

'No,' he said quickly, shaking his head with force. 'No way. I'm going away. Far away.'

'Aha,' I said. 'Why?'

He shrugged his shoulders, as if he thought it a stupid question, not worthy of an answer.

'Are you not happy here?' I asked.

He stood and walked over to the open door where he placed himself on the threshold with one hand on either side of the doorframe. It looked as if he was pushing hard. He had his back towards me and he said nothing. I waited.

'Are you sad now?' he said finally without turning around, ignoring my question. 'Are you sad when you are here?'

I considered the question for a moment before I answered.

'No, I'm not sad. I'm a kind of happy. A little happy in a sad way.'

He remained where he was and I could see the muscles on his back playing. For some reason he was still pushing hard against the doorframe.

'Come and sit here at the table,' I said, 'and I'll tell you about other places where I have lived.'

He took his time but eventually he returned and sat down across from me.

And so we talked about other places.

I think we were both relieved to change the subject.

4.

Someone once shrugged off something I had told him, saying that such things didn't happen in real life. That it was too far-fetched to be believable. But far-fetched things do happen. In fact, many people's entire lives are completely far-fetched. I think we are constantly surrounded by extraordinary possibilities. Whether we are aware of them or not, whether we choose to act on them or not, they are there. What is offered to us that we choose not to act upon falls by the wayside, and the road that is our life is littered with rejected, ignored and unnoticed opportunities, good and bad. Chance meetings and coincidences become extraordinary only when acted upon. Those that we allow to pass us by are gone forever. We never know where they might have taken us. I think they were never meant to happen. The potential was there, but only for the briefest moment, before we consciously or unconsciously chose to ignore it.

As I was slowly becoming aware of my growing sense of restlessness I had also come to think that human bodies are brought together as if by gravity, or by some other kind of natural law unknown to me. We are helpless and unable to resist. Gathered or separated by a power that has nothing to do with our own will. If we could view ourselves from above we would observe an intricate pattern emerging: a chain of minute incidents and developments, seemingly random, but all part of a coherent process with an ultimate goal. Or at least an end result of some kind. A reaction, if you like. As if a power beyond our control is using us in an experiment. Pushing us together in different combinations to see what will ensue.

When I stopped to reflect, I realised that everything that had ever happened in my life – even before my own life began – had contributed to bring me to where I now was, physically and emotionally. There is no such thing as a considered choice. That was what I had come to think. There had been a time when I would have argued the opposite with passion. Believed it. But not any more. No, now I had come to believe that at the moment we make our decision, it is clear it is the only option. I could fool myself into believing there were choices, but they were only mine until the moment I made my decision. There is no going back in time, and there are no opportunities to change anything. So the idea of free choice no longer had any meaning for me. I no longer believed in it. I had concluded that there was no such thing. I could possibly learn from experience and in that manner adjust my response to a future situation. I wasn't even sure that was true. Few people seem to learn from experience. And nobody can ever change a single action of the past.

I don't think my changed view had anything to do with a longing for forgiveness.

Or perhaps it did. But it was only my own forgiveness I needed.

At the time when the pivotal incidents of my life took place, I had seen life very differently. Then, I saw myself as a person who had choices, and made conscious decisions about them, and who was therefore also fully responsible for her actions. There was nobody to help me understand that they were not considered decisions at all, but instinctive reactions to circumstances imposed on me, for which I could in no way be held responsible. Perhaps what I was now trying to do was give myself some peace of mind by adjusting my perspective. I wanted a sort of moral amnesty, which only I could grant myself.

It wasn't that I was unwilling to accept responsibility for my actions. I had always carried an absolute sense of responsibility, and an overwhelming sense of guilt. But now I wanted to teach myself forgiveness.

I wasn't aware of any conscious analysis of the events that had brought me to this point. Yet I realised that they lived inside me, all the moments of my life. Significant as well as insignificant, they were there, in their separate boxes. I had been careful to keep them at the back of my mind. I had suppressed them, in a sense, but I had lived with a constant awareness of their weight. I had worried sometimes that I would forget. That I would begin to doubt my memory. So from time to time I had allowed myself a glimpse. Just to make sure they were all there. That I remembered.

However clear my memories were, I was aware that there was more to each one than I could ever recall. That there existed other, equally valid perspectives. And that those who might have been able to offer other points of view were no longer here. I could never know their observations, hear their interpretations. Their memories, irrevocably intertwined with mine, were forever out of reach. I knew that I didn't own the complete truth, but what I had was all there was. So I guarded my memories and my truths, such as they were. Held on to them with a kind of desperation. Like a film cut into a number of individual stills I kept the images at the back of my mind. I needed to be able to access the beginning, to keep it in mind. So that I would be able to tolerate the other images. Live with them. Own them.

Because they were there. All the stills.

My life in pictures, locked up in their respective sealed boxes.

5.

Ika's question during that early meal together awakened memories. Some of those on which I seldom dwelled. Those that sat at the furthermost back of my mind as an ever-present background murmur, a sea forever undulating in a constrained dark place. Never visible, yet always there. Those memories coloured everything. In a sense, they were the reason I lived where I lived, did what I did. Perhaps they were my reason for living. I carried them in my thoughts and in my dreams, but never as a shape or form, only as a fragrance, a colour, a mood, that in its elusiveness yet seemed like a prerequisite for everything else. In a way, living with those memories felt similar to living with my heart: I trusted them to be there and support me, but I rarely gave them a conscious thought.

After Ika had left that day I walked down to the beach, and I allowed myself to think. I thought about the journey. How I came to land here on the other side of the earth.

Almost fifteen years ago. I was thirty-six years old. It was February, still summer. I don't know what made me choose this country and this particular place. Perhaps it was the sheer distance. A need to remove myself as far away as possible from my previous life. I could not remember much of the process that had carried me here. It felt as if the time between the moment I stood barefoot on the tiled bathroom floor in a house in London, and the sensation of the warm sand under my feet and a blindingly bright light in my eyes here on this beach, had dissolved. It was as if the scenes had been cut from the film and discarded.

I did remember waking up one day and realising I had no wish to live. Or perhaps I just didn't want to continue the life I was living.

I looked at the man with whom I had shared my home for eight years and I realised I didn't know him at all, and that I no longer wanted to. I recognised every feature of his face where it rested still on the pillow beside me, eyes closed. I took it in but the sight evoked no emotional response. If I felt anything at all it was a kind of subdued sadness. And a sense of mild compassion. For him, and perhaps for me. For our lives. He looked so innocent and vulnerable, asleep beside me in our bedroom in the house we had bought with such anticipation, renovated with such energy.

I listened to the sounds that surrounded us. The hum of the awakening traffic in the street outside our window, the morning paper landing on the hallway floor, the closing of a car door. The familiar sounds of a city waking up. But suddenly I realised they were no longer a comfortable backdrop to my daily life, but identifiable, individual sounds that had nothing to do with comfort; rather the opposite. Just like the man beside me, the signs of life outside seemed to have nothing to do with me. Or perhaps it was I who had stepped outside the surrounding world. I could suddenly see and hear it all with acute clarity.

Later, as we sat in the kitchen, each with a section of the morning paper in front of us, I again looked at his face across the table. He had aged, I noticed. There were small wrinkles at the corners of his eyes and the one across his forehead was deeper than I remembered. His hair was thinning. It was an attractive face, yet curiously alien. I kept looking, searching for an emotional response. In him. And in myself. He must have felt my gaze, because he looked up and gave a surprised quick smile. Instantly I could see that he was unused to my interest, and it made me sad to realise this.

I saw my solicitor a few days later. Then I walked into a travel agency and booked my flight. Not that same day, but shortly after, as a logical consequence. With hindsight it seemed very swift, as if it had been carefully planned for a long time. Perhaps it was just the passage of time that made it feel like that. My mind working to compress this long period into a tiny shard. A concentrate of a substantial part of my life. Thousands of mornings, days and nights reduced to just a few scenes.

I was married to this man for eight years, and I had known him for three years before that. Eleven years of my life. Our separation was what is usually called amicable. I find it a strange term. Certainly there was no animosity. Little feeling of any kind, in fact. But amicable? I think he felt as I did – just a vague sense of sadness at the futility of it all. We were able to sort out our affairs without conflict. Perhaps that is what constitutes an amicable separation. It was defined not by the presence of friendship but the lack of animosity. And then he walked out of my life, leaving nothing behind. Or rather we just walked in different directions, leaving our shared life to dissolve behind us. Not one leaving the other, just the two separating, taking different routes forwards. After the odd sporadic contact as practical matters required us to talk, there was nothing. Yet there had been a time when I loved him. There must have been. I thought about him as I let my feet sink into the soft sand and I tried to recall my feelings. But all I could hear were my conscious justifications: his good looks, kindness, sense of humour, loyalty. I could remember the years when we tried so hard to start a family. The shared sadness at the inevitable monthly disappointment.

But love? No, I could not remember love.

Not now that I knew what love was.

It was still painful for me to recall what followed. But over time the memories had taken on a different quality. Or perhaps rather my way of living with them. It was as if the happiness that preceded the inevitable end didn't quite shine with the energy required to penetrate. That changed. But it was painful then.

I groped for my memories. The most important ones. The most precious ones. I thought about my arrival, and the film slowed down until the pace was unbearably slow. It was as if it wanted to ensure that it would be able to stop before it had carried on too far, to that part my memory had learnt to avoid. So the film that contained my memories kept returning to the beginning, like a scratched disc. I could view my arrival here, but that was as far as I was able to get. The consequences of my impulsive journey to the other side of the earth were still hidden.

I wasn't able to reach the memory of my jubilant joy, the intense colours and the feeling of absolute freedom. The love. Instead, as I sat there on the beach that day I still saw everything through the filter I had created in order to survive. I could not see the happiness that preceded the abyss. I had forced myself to keep this memory suppressed, forced myself not to acknowledge my life's most splendid moment, in order to be able to live out the rest of my life without it. I think that was what had happened. It has changed since, but back then it was impossible for me to embrace the happiness I had lost.

I had driven from Auckland in the early afternoon. I took my time, for several reasons. I wanted to find a new, slower rhythm. And I wanted the foreign landscape to come alive. I wanted to take the time to see how the changing light shifted the hue on the green hills. Take in the vastness of the sky. And finally that of the sea. I wanted to own the sense of infinity that the sea offered. I wanted to find a way back to life.

And so I had slowed down, driven off the road onto the dry sandy grass and parked. Why there? Why at that exact moment?

I tried to inspect my travels from a higher perspective. A dispassionate and objective view. And from above it looked strange: the taxi through the busy streets of north London and on to Heathrow. The anonymous flight to Singapore and two nights in an equally anonymous hotel. Surrounded by people and no doubt by innumerable possibilities, yet contained in a space of my own. Then the flight to Auckland: one long sleep cocooned in a capsule racing through the air. Another hotel. Sightseeing. The human intercourses I experienced brief and impersonal. Yet logically, there must have been many situations with more promise.

But it was here, on the deserted beach that stretched before me now, that I came to stop.

Before stepping out of the car she removes first her earrings, then her watch and the clasp that holds her hair together. Then her shoes. She needs to rid herself of all that connects her with the person she was. Shed the past. Here she is, dressed in her light cotton dress and nothing else. She has the car keys in her hand, but that is all she carries. As she descends the snaking ladder that leads down to the beach the breeze blows her hair and lifts her skirt. At the bottom she stops in the shade of the trees, looking out over the beach and the sea.

She is still Marion Flint. Yet not the one she used to be. She is still thirty-six years old. She has been here on the other side of the world just a few days. Yet the old world is fading fast. Something new is beginning. Here, by herself, in an environment that doesn't acknowledge her presence, she finally feels a kind of hope. She can breathe. That is how it feels. As if she were born just now, just here, and released of all that has been before.

The vast beach lies in front of her. There is not a person in sight. In the distance, the air quivers over the mirror created by the latest withdrawing wave. She stands still, her feet deep in the warm sand. It is as if this is where she wants to be forever. To see the world as it appears at this exact moment.

I am just a speck. A grain of sand, she thinks.

She starts to walk towards the water. The sand is very hot and she has to run to reach the sea. She lets the waves lap against her legs, and even here, with the water only up to her shins, she can feel the pull as the sand is dragged away around her feet. She bends down and wets her hands, and puts the palms on her cheeks. The water is cool against her skin and salty on her tongue.

She walks along the edge of the water. The roar of the sea fills the air and the only sound that penetrates is the odd shriek of a bird. There are no smells other than the sea. No other visual impressions. It is as if the sea occupies all her senses. She is completely enveloped by it, as insignificant as the shells that roll in the surf.

She carries on, keeping to the cool wet sand near the sea. Stops here and there to pick up a smooth pebble or a polished shell. She walks much further than she had intended, letting the breeze tousle her hair and the salt spray set on her skin. The beach is endless, one smooth bay following the next. And no sign of any human presence.

Eventually she slows down, and when she spots a large log lying further up the beach she heads for it. Again, she has to run over the hot sand.

It is not until she almost stumbles on it that she sees it. And for a split second her brain leaves the visual impression to be interpreted by the part that has hitherto spotted stones and shells. The part of her brain that has noticed the beauty of the towering waves and the sweeping surf. Shapes and forms, light and colour.

For that brief moment it is a natural object of beauty, nothing else.

But it is a man's body. And it is naked.

It is a man lying face down on a beach towel with a camera bag beside him.

He must have felt her presence because he wakes with a start, twisting to look at her without turning over. She takes a few steps back.

'I am so sorry, I just didn't see you,' she says. Which is partly true.

He is busy trying to wrap the beach towel around himself before struggling to his feet.

'Ah . . .' he says, stumbling a little before standing in front of her with the towel around his hips. 'Well, I'm sorry too. I thought I was alone here.'

Then he smiles.

He is tanned; obviously spends time outdoors. His hair is bleached by the sun, almost white. Curly, nearly reaching his shoulders.

'Turn around and let me put my shorts on,' he says, and she obliges, lifting one foot then the other on the hot sand.

'I was heading for the log over there,' she says, and starts off towards it, a few metres away. She sits down on the log and lifts her feet off the sand as he approaches and sits beside her. He holds out a bottle of water, which she accepts. She had not realised how thirsty she is. The cool water trickles over her chin and drips onto her chest.

He watches, smiling.

'Never leave home without your water bottle,' he says. 'That, and sunblock. Essential here.'

He is not a Kiwi. American, perhaps.

'Oh, I didn't mean to walk this far,' she says. 'I just wanted to get out of the car for a while. But then I started to walk along the sea, and somehow I just carried on . . .'

He looks out to sea.

'It's easy to be carried away here. It sort of feels like you have the world to yourself. As if anything is possible.'

Now it is her turn to smile. And she nods. Because that is exactly how it feels.

His name is Michael. That is not how he spells it, but she doesn't know this yet.

He is a photographer. From Canada. On a job here.

What can she tell him? Who is she?

'My name is Marion,' she says. She knows that much for certain. 'Marion Flint. I'm here on a holiday, I suppose it is. A kind of holiday. Or a kind of hiatus. A pause in my life. Between one life and another.'

'By yourself?' he asks, and she nods.

'I just needed some time to myself . . .' She does not look at him.

He makes no comment.

'Do you mind if I take a few shots?' he asks.

She laughs self-consciously.

'Of me?'

He is already unpacking the camera. It looks expensive and professional. She pulls her skirt down over her legs and hugs them.

'Don't look at me,' he says. 'Forget I'm here. Stay in that world of yours. Watch the sea.'

All the while he talks about his project. He is at the tail end of a nation-wide tour, trying to capture life in the most isolated places along the coast. He hopes his pictures will portray the people who live in the outermost parts of the country, in the most distant places where land and sea meet. Those who live by the untameable sea, and off it.

'A few years ago, I followed Norwegian trawlers in the North Sea. It's not the sea I am interested in, it's the people who have allowed the sea to guide their lives. Who have managed to create a life on the terms of the sea. To me, that's a little bit like embracing a spiritual or religious faith.

A faith in something infinitely bigger than you and completely beyond your control. It takes courage to let go of yourself, accept that you are in the hands of something bigger. They fascinate me, these people. And I try to capture them in my pictures.'

He lowers the camera with a smile and a shrug.

'It probably makes no sense.'

He returns the lens cap and puts the camera back in its bag.

'Are you hungry?' he asks, as if to change the topic.

And she realises she is.

'Yes, I really should head back to my car,' she says, and stands up.

'Mine is probably closer,' he says. 'Just up there, beyond the dunes. If you can eat barbecued crayfish with bread and salad, you're most welcome to share my lunch.'

They run quickly over the hot sand. The soles of her feet are burning but she feels light, as if carried on the wind.

'Here, take this,' he says as they reach his car. He holds out a faded sunhat. The four-wheel drive is parked in the shade of a large tree. 'You should be careful, the sun is dangerous here. Put it on. And turn around.'

She does and he rubs sunblock on her back and shoulders. His hand gently lifts her hair to reach her neck.

Who am I? she thinks. Who is this person who stands here, barefoot on a beach, allowing a stranger to rub her back and shoulders? Her neck and her arms? She smiles – can't help herself. She can't possibly be me. She is new and the world is new.

'It's a pohutukawa,' he says, pointing upwards. 'This tree that shades us. A month earlier and it would have been covered in red flowers. It's odd, but like jacaranda flowers they are hard to photograph. Never come out quite as extraordinary as the real thing. But I guess that goes for many things . . .'

He takes out a low folding chair for her, and she sits and watches him get the small barbecue going. He squats on the ground before her and while he is busying himself, he tells her about his long and winding journey through

31

the country, from the Far North all the way down to Bluff and Stewart Island. And then back up along the West Coast. His back is tanned and tiny drops of sweat glisten along his spine.

He looks up and asks her where she has been.

'Oh, nowhere really. I've just arrived.'

He nods and takes the lid off the chilly-bin he has unpacked from the car.

The crayfish is enormous. It looks like a large lobster, she thinks. And it's alive. He holds it up, laughing. She asks if she can use his camera and he nods. When she has it ready he poses happily holding the crayfish in his hand. Then he takes out a knife, holds the crayfish down on a piece of driftwood and kills it with a swift insertion of the knife in the neck. She is not sure if crayfish can be considered to have necks. The crayfish flounders a couple of times, then it is still. He splits it lengthwise and puts the two halves face down on the barbecue. While it cooks he makes a salad, wraps some bread in tinfoil and places it on the barbecue. All the while he rejects her offers of help. And all the while she keeps taking pictures. The powerful zoom takes her close to his face while he focuses on what he is doing. She clicks away. Picture after picture.

'I've done this for so long, it's a routine that can't be altered,' he says, smiling. 'I enjoy doing it myself. But don't let this fool you. This is the only cooking I do. I am hopeless in a normal kitchen.'

She laughs. She can hear the sound of her own laughter. It flows from inside her like the most natural thing. Where is it coming from? She is not aware of having heard it ever before.

They sit side by side in the low chairs, facing the sea and with their plates on their laps. The chilly-bin sits between them and on it are two cold beers.

She still has a feeling of floating, of not quite touching the ground. She closes her eyes against the sun.

Then she looks at him. She is not aware of having any thoughts at all. She is all lightness and light.

'Why don't you join me for the last leg of my trip?' he says suddenly.

'It's just for a couple of days. I have to be back in Auckland next week. I'll show you something you wouldn't find by yourself.'

She is helpless; she has nothing to hold her back.

'If we're lucky the godwits will still be around.'

'Godwits?'

'Here they are called kuaka. They're a wading bird. They migrate here from Alaska every year, and then back at the end of summer. The longest non-stop bird migration there is. Apparently they cruise on the winds and manage without food or water all the way, up to ten days or more. Because they are wading birds they can't feed out on the sea. They have to reach land. A very risky undertaking, it seems to me. But somehow they manage it, year after year.'

He looks out over the sea and she studies his profile.

'But that's not why I want to see this place. It's the place itself. That isolated peninsula ruled by the sea. I want to explore it. Feel it.'

He pauses.

'It would be great if you came.'

'Yes,' she hears herself say. 'Yes, I would like that. I would like that very much.'

He turns and looks at her, a wide smile spreading over his face.

'Great! That's settled then. Let's pack up, and go and get your car. The roads are narrow and winding and it will take us a while to get to Kawhia. There are a couple of motels there and we can have a decent meal. And a shower. But from there on we'll have to camp. Are you okay camping?'

She has never camped before, but she feels as if she can do anything.

So she nods. Yes, camping will be fine.

Nothing could be better.

6.

I was jumping ahead. Like a child who picks the brightest, most tempting Christmas present first, I had picked this memory. But there was so much that came before. So much that needed to fall into place for it all to become a coherent whole.

It was getting late and I realised he was not coming. I would be eating soup for days. I didn't mind, but for some reason I felt a little restless. I took the pot off the stove, got my windbreaker from the hook by the door and grabbed my camera, which always lay handy on the dresser by the front door. The white light was greying as a weak setting sun tried to penetrate low cloud. I walked briskly, a little cold at first. The beach was empty as far as my eyes could see. The odd gannet and seagull were the only signs of life. I aimed my camera at them and took a few shots. I wondered why – I had innumerable such shots. But there was something about the late afternoon light here that was irresistible. That, and the sight of the carefree, peaceful passage of birds across the sky. My futile hope of capturing the very essence of this moment. The tide was out and the packed sand was cool under my feet.

Watching the sea through the viewfinder I thought about what it had come to stand for. Coherence. To me, the sea had come to represent coherence. Wholeness. And resilience, perhaps. The sea allowed other elements to influence it temporarily, but it remained its own self. I longed for that kind of resilience. For a sense of wholeness. I wanted to know that whatever lay in store for me I would be able to remain myself. My whole self, containing everything I had ever been, and everything I had the potential to become.

I sat down at the edge of the grass. My eyes set on the sweeps of water that smoothed the sand in front of me and I clicked away, one similar yet different image after another. There was nothing on that beach that reminded me of anything else, anywhere else. It seemed to be absolutely itself, and eternal. Perhaps that was the attraction of it. This place didn't belong to me and it never would. My brief existence here would leave no traces at all. Yet when my eyes moved out to sea and followed the creation of one of the giant waves – watched it rise out of the deceptively smooth dark sea, rise higher and higher till it reached its impossible shimmering perilous climax, where it seemed to balance for a fraction of a second before violently breaking with a deafening thunder – I could feel how closely tied to this environment I had become. How much of my life belonged here. If not in time, then certainly in significance. It was here that my life's equivalent of that shimmering climax took place. My life's triumphant moment of unreserved love.

Yet all that came before it took place so very far away, just like the gathering of momentum of the waves.

Such a long, slow build-up.

Such an evanescent climax.

And such an endless aftermath.

I stood up and resumed my walk. I needed to go back, sift through my memories for the beginning. I needed to understand the whole. Follow the build-up from its origin.

I groped for my first conscious memory, made a concerted effort to work myself backwards in time. It felt odd, because as the memories drifted past I realised there were many more than I had ever imagined. They rewound like a slow-motion film, coming into focus then fading away again.

Until finally the film came to a stop. My first memory. I tried not to look, but to get inside it. I tried to be that little girl again.

She was so small. I could suddenly see that. In my memory she had seemed older. But now I was able to watch her with tenderness and embrace her smallness.

And see how vulnerable she was.

She walks behind her grandfather. She is barefoot, just like him. They walk slowly. Every now and then he stops and turns, sometimes to hold a branch out of the way, tear away a cobweb. Sometimes just to smile.

As the trees clear, they step out onto the sun-warm red rocks. It is still and the sun is warm on her skin. Grandfather turns again. She expects a smile. She is already smiling in anticipation. But there is no smile. Instead, Grandfather abruptly picks her up and his grip is tight, hurting under her arms as he hoists her into the air. She reaches for his neck and holds on hard as he takes a few quick steps and jumps up onto the planks of the landing. She can feel his heartbeat under the warm skin of his chest, hear his rapid breathing. He stands still for a moment, catching his breath.

Then slowly he sets her down again, straightens her sundress and takes her hand. He crouches beside her and points to the rocks below. There are little drops of sweat on his forehead. His grip on her hand is too tight and she tries to prise her hand loose. In response his grip softens and she lets her hand remain in his.

'There, Marianne,' he whispers, his eyes on the smooth rock that they have just left. She doesn't like Grandfather whispering.

'Can you see it?' He waits for her to nod. She can see it. It looks like a long thin sausage that is slowly uncoiling, grey against the reddish-grey rock and difficult to spot. Glistening in the sun now and soundlessly gliding over the smooth surface. She can see the dark zigzag band that runs along its back.

'That's a snake,' he says. Then he pauses, as if he needs to think a little. 'Beautiful, isn't it?' Again he waits, and she understands that he is waiting for her to agree. She doesn't think it's beautiful but she nods again.

'But if you scare it, it might bite you.' The slowness of grandfather's speech is frightening: every pause, every moment of hesitation bringing her closer to tears.

'Snakes are very shy,' he continues. 'Very easily frightened. They should be left alone.'

He takes hold of both her hands and turns her to face him. He looks into her eyes. She doesn't like it. It feels as if something is wrong, and Grandfather can't make it right again.

'If ever you see one, just walk quietly away. Will you remember that, Marianne?' She nods. Swallows hard. But she can no longer hold back the tears.

'You're not afraid, are you?' Grandfather says and runs his rough palm over her cheeks to wipe away the tears. She shakes her head but she is not sure. 'There's no reason to be. Just leave them alone.' He smiles. And she nods. But somewhere inside she is scared now. Because she can sense that Grandfather is.

'Good girl. All you have to remember is to take care not to scare snakes. Always look where you walk. We must give snakes their space and they will let us have ours.'

He lifts her up again and now his hands are soft and gentle. As they usually are. She presses her face into his neck. He holds her in his arms as he sits down on the landing, then slides into the dinghy.

And everything is back to normal. She can smell the sun on her grandfather's chest. He smiles as he sets her down and takes hold of the oars. But she can still see the sweat on his forehead.

'Let's row across the bay. And when we get back home we'll have raspberry cordial and rusks.' He smiles and the oars make soft little splashes as he begins to row.

But there is a snake on the rocks behind them.

Now, why this single scene? I must have been almost four. I turned four in September that year and this was early summer. Of all the days of my early childhood, this was what came to my mind. Why had I saved this? I remembered vividly every detail of it. Yet nothing that came before.

I remembered how my grandfather's hands felt. The pang of surprise at his tight grip under my arms. The rapid breathing near my ear. In an instant he was changed. Irrevocably different. My entire world was changed. Abruptly, it had come to contain things that could frighten the one person who had always made my world safe. And if he was afraid, so was I.

I searched for other early memories.

I searched for my mother. The search took me through many boxes, many rooms. Elusive, she seemed to be everywhere and nowhere, an all-permeating fragrance rather than a body. She was there, but I

38

couldn't hold on to her long enough to see her clearly. She came and went, disappeared around corners. It was her absence I remembered more than her presence.

Until that final scene. I knew I could see her there, but I wanted other pictures. Other memories, earlier. It was a timeline I was after. One scene, one memory at a time. In the right order.

As I searched, another scene emerged. And I could see that it was connected of course. Here, I was five, almost six. The two years separating the scenes had left no traces, it seemed. But perhaps this was the beginning. The origin of all that was to come. Perhaps that was why it was emerging so clearly. Perhaps I had saved it because it represented the beginning.

It seemed to me that despite my lack of conscious overview, some kind of mechanism in my mind must have selected and saved some memories and discarded others. For at the time when these events took place I could not possibly have been aware of their significance.

The five-year-old who could not quite reach the window without standing on a stool could have had no idea of what was to follow. Not that anybody else could have either. But in hindsight it was there to see, sharply and clearly. Till that day, I had lived in a world where place was a given and time didn't exist. Abruptly, here I came to understand that there was an outside.

Perhaps it was natural for me to remember the moment that propelled me outside.

She stands by the upstairs bedroom window and waits for her mother to arrive. She is too short to see without standing on something. She has prepared herself, pushed up a chair and climbed onto it. She must have known that Mother was coming. She is tense. Not with excitement: it is an

instinctive reaction to an undefined threat. She is perched there, waiting. Has she been here for a long time? Perhaps. It feels like a long time. It is a still and sunny day, and a fly is trapped inside the window. It is buzzing as it slowly crawls along the window ledge, and every now and then it makes a tired attempt to fly, shorter each time. She waits, more and more anxious. She needs to pee, but she can't leave now. She can hear a car, though she can't yet see it.

When she finally sees Mother appear by the gate her throat begins to hurt. It feels as if something is stuck inside and she tries to swallow, but it doesn't help. She really needs to pee. She presses her thighs together to try to hold it back. She has to stay here, has to keep watching. Her mother looks strange from up here. She can see the top of her head but she can't see her face. She knows it is her mother, of course. But it doesn't feel right. Something is terribly wrong. It's not like other visits. This time is different. And she has to stand here and watch, though she doesn't want to.

She knows that Mother is smiling as she closes the gate behind her, even if she can't see her face. But the smile is all over Mother, in the way she moves. The new red dress. The matching red shoes. Inside the gate she sets her small brown suitcase down on the grass, and as she stands she gathers her blonde hair with one hand and lifts her face towards the sun. Now she can see the smile. Mother closes her eyes to the sun and she smiles and smiles. The wind catches the wide skirt of her dress and it balloons around her. She doesn't think Mother can see her, and she doesn't wave. She keeps her fingers clasped around the edge of the windowsill and her forehead touches the glass. Mother picks up the suitcase, and she keeps smiling as she begins to walk up the gravel path, balancing precariously in her high-heeled shoes. She looks light and beautiful and she swings her white handbag back and forth.

The little girl watches, still. The fly has stopped moving too. It lies on its back with its legs in the air. She can hear the gravel crunch as Mother carries on up the path towards the porch.

Suddenly she feels like crying. She slides down onto the floor and skids on the shiny floorboards as she runs across the landing. She can't hold back any longer and she can feel pee trickling down the insides of her thighs. She can't hold back the tears either. She hurries downstairs as quickly as she can, holding on to the handrail. Runs across the downstairs hallway and into the kitchen as if her life depended on it. Grandfather sits at the table with the paper spread in front of him. Without taking his eyes off the page he stretches out one arm and whisks her up onto his lap as she comes running. Grandfather doesn't seem to care that her panties are wet, so she doesn't either. She buries her nose in the shirt that smells of Grandfather. He strokes her arm with his rough palm. He must know too, but he says nothing. It is as if they are both pretending they can't hear the light steps outside, first on the gravel, then up the wooden steps, across the porch. Over the threshold and through the open door. Grandfather's eyes stay on the paper and he keeps stroking her arm. Even when she can smell Mother's perfume she continues to keep her eyes closed and her face buried in the folds of Grandfather's shirt. She doesn't want to see the smile. She doesn't want to see the new dress.

She can hear her mother pull out a chair and she can hear the skirt rustle as she sits down.

And as Mother speaks, Grandfather's grip around her waist tightens, as does hers around his neck. They are holding on to each other like two drowning people.

'I've come to collect Marianne,' her mother says.

7.

I stood up, brushed the sand off my trousers and carried on along the beach. The slight overcast that had hidden the sun all day had finally dissolved, and the sunset painted the remaining thin clouds a greyish purple now. I knew that the images I captured would be pale copies of the real moments, but I took a few more shots. I continued further than I had intended and I turned the camera to the sea again and again. There was nothing to see except the rolling waves.

The lens swept over the empty surface of the sea, and suddenly it caught a small speck on the undulating water behind the surf. I don't know what made me notice the tiny object, but I started running before I was consciously aware of its significance. I dropped the camera and tore off my jacket as I rushed towards the edge of the water. It seemed to take an eternity before I reached water deep enough to begin to swim. I dived under the surf and finally emerged in deeper water. My eyes frantically scanned the surface. I was already very cold, and not just because of the chill of the water. My whole body felt frozen from the inside. Only when I finally spotted him could I breathe again. He wasn't far from me now and as I took the last few strokes and my hand finally touched his hair I could not help myself from screaming. I kept shouting his name, but I could hardly hear myself over the thunder of the waves that kept breaking just beyond us. We rose and fell, carried by the enormous energy below. I held him against my chest and he seemed weightless as I started backstroking towards the beach. He made no move, didn't resist but lay limp against my body. I knew it meant he was unconscious.

When my feet touched ground again, I stood and lifted him in my arms and waded through the water. When I reached dry sand I ran. I put him down and started working. His lips were cold and he lay still with his arms outstretched as they had fallen, but I could feel his heartbeat under my hands. I put my lips against his and continued to fill his lungs with my breath, until finally his chest contracted in a spasm and he drew a first rasping breath and coughed. I turned him on his side and watched as seawater poured from his mouth. I waited till it subsided, then turned him onto his back again and kneeled waiting for a moment, my hands resting on his chest. His eyes remained closed. When his breathing was even I wrapped him in my jacket, slung my camera over my shoulder, lifted him up and hurried back to my house.

I could hear myself weep and moan as I went.

Inside, I put him down on the sofa in the living room. He looked so small, much younger now with his eyes closed and his body limp, than in his normal active state. I hesitated a moment before I began to remove his wet clothes. From the early stages of our relationship I had instinctively realised he didn't like to be touched. Only a few times – when I had had to treat his hair for lice, or dress a cut – had I ever been allowed to touch him, and I had been very careful to make him understand that I respected his need for distance. He shied away from even the most casual touch.

But here I was gently pulling off his T-shirt and exposing his skinny chest. I could count the ribs. I pulled the shirt over his head and gently laid his head to rest on the cushion, then I stopped abruptly and my hands fell into my lap.

I looked down on the small child.

And I began to cry again. Unable to stop myself, I kept whispering under my breath, 'No, oh no.' I squeezed the balled-up T-shirt in my hands.

There were dark bruises underneath his arms, as if someone had lifted him violently. Around his neck, as if someone had tried to strangle him. I bent forwards and gently turned him onto one side. There was a large dark bruise on the torso, over the kidney. And there were faint older bruises beside the fresh ones.

I had seen such bruises before, and I knew these had not happened in the sea. Nor were they a result of my resuscitation efforts. No, these were the marks of adult hands, an adult foot. Intentional abuse of the small body.

I stood up and went to fetch the camera. Turned on the floor-lamp by the sofa. My hands shook as I took off the lens cap. But as I lifted the camera a strange calmness filled me, and I carefully took all the pictures I knew I had to take. I had turned on the date feature, ensuring that all the pictures would be dated.

As soon as I finished and turned off the light I began to cry again. By now it was almost dark. I pulled the blanket up over him and watched his face. He looked peaceful and his breathing was calm. I was overcome by a strong impulse to put my lips against his forehead and whisper that all would be fine. That I would make it so. But all I did was run my finger slowly along the arm that rested on the blanket. His skin was dry and cool and crusted with salt. A shudder rocked my body and I realised I was very cold myself. I needed to change too, but I didn't want to leave him. I stood and lifted him in my arms, carried him into my bedroom and tucked him in. I watched him for a moment. He lay still, eyes closed. His hair had dried in spikes that stuck out from his head. Somehow the sight made me upset again. It was as if this added further to the look of utter vulnerability. I left the door open when I went out to put the kettle on and change into dry clothes.

Later I sat at the kitchen table with a mug of tea trying to sort my tumultuous thoughts. I had never enquired about his family, other than to ensure that they knew where he was when he was at my house. He had never volunteered any information, just nodded or shaken his head in response to my questions. I realised now that I knew nothing about his life.

There must be someone I should ring. Someone who would be worried. Someone who must have missed him by now. It was late and darkness was falling rapidly.

The professional part of me must have known what to do, but there was a primitive part that refused to listen. A part of me that instinctively just wanted to protect him. Make sure he was safe. And never let him out of my sight again.

Yet I knew that I could not just keep him without letting the family know. It was just not possible.

I didn't even know his surname, and I only had a vague idea where he lived.

I returned to the living room and dropped down on the sofa, wrapping a blanket around me. As if he sensed that I was cold, Kasper jumped up and lay down beside me.

I had no idea what to do.

Finally I picked up the phone and rang George. I don't know why.

I don't know what I was hoping to achieve, but I rang him. He took a while to answer and when he did he sounded hesitant, as if the sound of the phone had surprised him. Over the years I had rung him a dozen times at the most. And never in the evening. Almost all our previous communications had been face to face. So this felt distinctly awkward to begin with. But George listened and asked no questions. I volunteered only the bare facts. That I had found Ika in the sea. That he was asleep and would be better off staying with me overnight. And that I didn't know whom to contact.

George knew who Ika was. I got the impression he knew about us, about our Thursday meals together, though he didn't say so. Perhaps it was common knowledge. What did I know? Again, I had that sense of being slightly handicapped, an outsider who hadn't quite grasped this community's unwritten rules of conduct. Others knew all about me, while I knew virtually nothing about them.

George also knew where Ika lived, knew of the family. Not that it was much of a family. Ika lived with his grandmother, apparently. George promised to drive over and talk to her, and then ring me back. I told him Ika was fine, and that I was happy to keep him overnight.

I went to the kitchen and made another cup of tea, turned on some music at low volume and returned to the sofa. I must have dozed off because I felt disoriented for a moment before I realised the phone was ringing.

George had talked to the grandmother. He cleared his throat and seemed to hesitate for a moment before he continued.

'She is not concerned. Happy for him to stay with you till tomorrow . . .' I felt that there was more he wanted to say, but he left the line silent.

'Should I call her, do you think?' I asked.

Again that awkward silence.

'No . . .' Pause. 'No, she doesn't expect you to.' Another pause. 'No need to ring.' Silence. 'I'll come over in the morning. I can take the boy home then, if you like.'

Somehow I got the feeling he didn't want me to meet the grand-mother. There were things I wanted to talk to her about, questions I wanted to ask. But I decided to leave it till the following day.

So, I just thanked him and hung up.

I tiptoed into the bedroom and checked on Ika. I stood at the foot of the bed and watched his face. He was lying on his back and his face was calm, his breath hardly audible. Now I thought he looked ancient. Like a person at the end of his life. Wise, as if he were above or beyond this world. I bent down and put my cheek on the blanket over his chest, let it brush against his cheek. It was dry and warm against mine.

I went back to the sofa, wrapped myself in the blanket again and fell into a deep sleep.

During the night I had the dream again.

It had been so long I thought it had finally left me.

It was the same, and yet it didn't feel the same at all. As always it was just the two of us, my brother and me. And once more I was surprised to see how young we were. At the time I might have thought that I was a big girl and fully aware of my responsibilities. But I was only about eight years old. My brother was so very little and he looked so sombre, too. There we were, alone, hand in hand, headed for the inescapable abyss.

She walks through the strip of forest down towards the water, her little brother by her side. The light is strange, as if a bright lamp were illuminating everything from above. Underneath the branches of the pines it is dark, but she is aware of the cold shadowless light beyond.

She is holding his hand. He is so small he has to reach up and his head is only just level with her waist. She has to walk very slowly to accommodate him, but she doesn't mind at all. If she could, she would stop altogether. As they get closer to the water she can smell it. It stinks of raw sewage. It is not summer, but not winter either. It is as no particular season, or a constant non-specific season that will never change. There are no other people around, just the two of them. They walk in silence, but it is a comfortable silence. There is love in it. But there is also a looming premonition of disaster. Her heart begins to pound. They reach the grey rocks that slope steeply down to the dark water. There is no wind at all. All is absolutely still. She is not looking up to the left but she knows it is there, the railway bridge arching high in the air.

For a brief moment, they balance on the edge of the rock, his small body touching her leg. The grey surface of the still sea looms far below, and despite the distance she can feel how cold it is. Colder than the air.

Suddenly he takes a step forwards, and even before it happens she knows that she will lose her grip on his hand. The little fingers slip from hers and he falls down the steep rock face and out of sight. It is eerily quiet. She can't hear a sound; the silence thunders in her ear.

Now everything slows down. She is paralysed and unable to make even the slightest move. Her eyes are fixed on the spot where she has seen him disappear. She can't hear him, but her whole body aches with every bump, every scratch the little body suffers on its ride down to the water. She is locked here, petrified and filled with an acute awareness that there is nothing she can do. In her head she goes through the awful sequence over and over, frozen and immobile. She is as scared as he must be. She hurts as he must. She is struggling to breathe. Nothing stirs.

Then, as if abruptly awakened from a trance, she turns and begins to run. Her steps feel heavy, and though her heart is racing her feet make painfully slow progress as she makes towards the bridge. It arches over her head, hopelessly out of reach. She finally stops at the foot of it and realises that there are no steps, nothing to hold on to. Just the smooth concrete foundation. It is impossible for her to climb. She looks up and realises that even if she could get up there, a jump down into the water would kill her.

At this instant she spots him in the water. And she is as cold as he must be. Shivering, she stares at his head, a dot on the still, leaden water.

And she knows it is too late.

She is so very cold, but she is no longer filled with the familiar paralysing dread. Instead, she is filled with the acute awareness that it is all over.

But this time the dream ends differently. It doesn't stop here.

No, this time she stands on the cliff and she feels the pain dissolve. It falls from her shoulders like a discarded garment.

Because she realises that she can let herself fall down the cliff too. And slowly she begins to walk towards the edge.

8.

The rapid tapping of the feet of a possum across the metal roof woke me. It was still dark. There were no sounds from the bedroom. I lay still, thinking. I had hoped to wake with a clear idea of what to do. I needed to talk to the grandmother, but of course this was likely to complicate things. I didn't know what to tell Ika, either. Nothing had cleared overnight.

I needn't have worried. It didn't really matter what decisions I made. What plans I might have. A chain of events had already been set in motion. And mostly the process was taking place inside me. Regardless of my conscious deliberations, my subconscious was already hard at work. It had its own strategy, as I would soon discover.

I must have been dozing again and I wasn't sure what woke me up this time because his steps were soundless. It was the awareness of his presence rather than a sound. I opened my eyes and my gaze landed on the small shape by the window. He stood there with his back to me, a silhouette against the cold morning light outside. He looked like a little tent with the folds of the blanket falling from his shoulders to the floor. When he heard me stir he walked slowly across the room, the blanket dragging behind him. He sat down on the floor near the sofa but so far away that I could not reach him. I waited for him to speak. He didn't.

'I'm glad you are here,' I said finally. Again, he said nothing.

'Are you warm?' He nodded. He had the blanket pulled tightly around his neck.

'Hungry?' He nodded.

So I got out of bed, pulled my woollen jersey over my nightgown and went to the kitchen.

'Soup okay?' I asked over my shoulder. I heard no response but then he appeared beside me at the bench, still holding on to the blanket with both hands. He remained there, silent, while I heated the soup and set the table.

We sat down. He struggled with the blanket while getting up onto the chair. It kept sliding down his shoulders. I made no attempt at helping, just tried to keep my eyes away from his neck. I served the soup and sliced bread. Poured a glass of milk. Holding on to the blanket with one hand, he began to eat. I watched as he finished the first bowl, and then served him a second.

When he had finally finished he leaned back on the chair, adjusting the blanket so that it reached his ears. It was as if he needed it as some kind of protection. Perhaps a shield against my probing eyes.

'Ika, I have to ask you a few things,' I said. He looked past me out the window and said nothing. It looked as if he shrank a little. And I felt moved to tears again. I didn't want to have this conversation, if it could be called that. I knew he would contribute precious little.

'What were you doing in the sea yesterday?' As I expected, he didn't respond. I was at a loss to know what to do. How to continue.

'It was Thursday and you knew I was here waiting for you,' I said, wincing at the sound of my words. I didn't want him to feel I was putting pressure on him. That his Thursday visits were an obligation. But there was no reaction, spoken or otherwise. He sat staring into space, immobile. I stood up and started to clear the table.

'If you don't tell me anything, I can't help you,' I said. I kept my back to him and my eyes on my hands as I cleared the last few pieces from the table and wiped it with a cloth.

'I think you need help. Everybody does from time to time. Some things are just too hard to deal with without help.'

I sat down at the table again. I couldn't help looking at him. I swallowed and began again.

'When I was about your age I thought I could manage by myself. But sometimes that just isn't possible. Some things are too hard for children to sort out.'

He still said nothing and refused to make eye contact.

'Can I ask you a few questions, Ika? You don't need to answer, just nod or shake your head. Okay?'

Nothing.

'Is that okay?' I repeated and bent forwards. He sat back, maintaining the distance between us. But I thought I could discern the slightest little nod. Or perhaps he just let his head sink lower to avoid my gaze.

'What were you doing in the sea yesterday? It's winter. The water is very cold.'

Nothing.

'Did you go into the sea because you were sad?'

A small shake of his head.

'Because you were scared?'

A nod. Possibly – it was hard to be sure.

'Did someone hurt you yesterday?'

A nod. A definite nod.

'Okay. You don't need to tell me what happened. But I would like to come with you to your home.'

Suddenly he looked up, not quite at me, but I could see his eyes widening, as if he were frightened. Terrified, in fact.

Vigorous shake of the head.

Did it mean he didn't want to go home? Or did it mean he didn't want me to accompany him?

I needed time to think. I had to take him home, or I had to report my suspicions. Possibly both. But it could not be done behind his back. I needed to try to explain something that was still muddled in my own head. So I bought us some time.

'Okay, let's think about it while we take showers and get dressed,' I said.

Which is what we did. We both showered, and I think we both thought.

I also thought about another little boy.

'Grow up!' she whispers. 'Please, grow up soon.'

She pushes down on the metal frame of the baby seat and lets it go. The little body bounces lightly against the soiled denim as the metal springs forwards, but the baby makes no sound. His unsmiling eyes stare back at her and he keeps sucking the first two fingers on his left hand as he rocks back and forth.

She presses down with more effort and lets go again, watching as he bounces a little harder, then slowly comes to rest. She bends forwards and puts her ear to his chest and feels a hushed, wheezy sound deep inside. It sounds like a fish sucking for air, she thinks. She knows how that sounds because she has been fishing with Grandfather. Before. Although that time is getting harder to see. She has to close her eyes to make the pictures appear and each time they seem a little duller. Smaller, too, as if watched from an ever-growing distance. She knows she needs them, though she tries not to think about them. Just occasionally to make sure they are still there. And each time she remembers she feels a rush of relief. She remembers. She remembers how the mouths of the fish looked. No lips, nothing like a mouth really, just white bony edges that kept opening and closing, while the round eyes stared at the sky. The gills that made no sound as they opened and closed in vain, exposing the strange blood-red membranes that slowly dried in the sun. Then a final sigh as the neck was snapped in Grandfather's hands. After that no sound, just the odd silent spasm until all was still. She does remember.

She bends forwards again and whispers into the soft ear that looks like a velvet shell.

'Grow up, please.' She pulls the baby fingers out of his mouth and waits, her eyes intently staring into his baby black ones. His eyes lock with hers, and he smiles and stretches a wet hand towards her.

'I love you,' she whispers, and takes the outstretched hand and sticks the pink little fingers into her own mouth.

9.

Ika came out of the bathroom wearing his shorts and T-shirt. I had put them to dry the night before but hadn't had time to wash them and they looked stiff and uncomfortable, saturated with dried salt. He walked over and sat down on the piano stool, his back to the piano, and stared into space.

'Ika, here is what I think we should do,' I said, trying to sound confident and hopeful.

'I think we should call Mr Brendel over the road and ask him to take us back to your home. He knows your grandmother.' Ika jumped and turned his face towards me, but as always without looking me in the eye. He said nothing.

'I will talk to your grandmother and we will see what to do,' I said, having no idea what I meant. What could be done, if anything.

Ika turned on the stool and put his hands on the keys.

I had discovered his musicality by chance. One Thursday I had sat down to play while I was waiting for him. My piano was never particularly good, and the humid and salty air in a house that was always more or less open to the elements had not been good for it. But it matched my ability rather well and I never had an audience. Or so I thought.

I had been listening to Bill Evans again. It had been a long time, and it wasn't until recently when I had finally mastered downloading music from the internet that I had found myself returning to music I used to love. I listened, and I was trying to teach myself to play some. But I ignored the echoes of the past that the music evoked.

That Thursday it was 'Peace Piece'. I was lost in the music, and hadn't noticed the hands on the windowsill outside. Suddenly a minute stirring caught my eye. I tried to keep my fingers moving over the keys and not break the atmosphere while I turned my head to see what he was doing. His dirty little hands were hanging on to the windowsill with such force that the nails shone white against the skin. I could only see a glimpse of the top of his head but I could see his hands. And that was when I first noticed that the third and fourth fingers on both hands were webbed. A fine, almost translucent film connected the two fingers from the base to the first joint. I hadn't noticed it before, but here the two hands were spread out in order to provide maximum support. My instant impression was of something exquisite and fragile. A mayfly's wings. Fins of a veil tail fish. Then my professional self took over, and I wondered if it was medically significant. I wracked my brain for information. Vague memories of various syndromes stirred, but I let them go, and focused on my playing again. When I finished and looked up the hands were no longer there.

'Come inside,' I called, still playing. 'Let's try the piano together.'

A moment later he appeared, and tentatively approached the piano.

I went to get another chair and indicated to him to sit on the piano stool. He did and I adjusted the height a little. I sensed that he thought that I was too close and I pulled my chair back a touch before I sat down.

'Have you seen a piano before?' I asked. He shook his head.

'Okay,' I said. 'Let me play some scales. It's a little bit like letting your fingers run up and down all the keys. Like this.'

Ika sat absolutely still watching my hands.

When I finished he tentatively put his own hands on the keys. He played the same scales, a little uncertainly, but hitting the right key almost every time. When he made the odd mistake he immediately corrected himself. Whatever I played, he played.

'Are you sure you have never seen a piano before?' I asked.

He shook his head, his eyes still focused on the keys.

I was utterly fascinated. In fact I was so moved I felt tears brimming in my eyes. I swallowed and leaned back on the chair.

And then he played 'Peace Piece'.

He had only heard me play it of course. So he played with my intonation, my hesitation. He stumbled here and there and he played with childish simplicity, but as I listened, I realised that he had corrected some of my mistakes. I wondered how long he had been hanging on the windowsill, and how many times before. I sat breathless, stunned.

After he finished we sat in silence for a moment. It felt as if our relationship had changed. As if we had all at once become closer. I also felt as if I had been given a new responsibility, one that I accepted without hesitation.

I realised he would come to need better teachers than I could ever be, but for a start, I could give him what I had to offer.

Since that first day he had gathered a strange repertoire. Initially I thought he just had an uncanny ability for memorising and copying. But there was more to his talent than that. He developed his own sound and his own interpretations. Always distinct, and utterly fascinating. And he had his own taste, unpredictable and diverse. I allowed it to meander, find its own way forwards. Often it felt like an adventure trail. We never knew where each piece would take us, to what new musical experience it would lead.

And here he was, again seated by the piano. I had no idea what he was thinking.

To allow me to collect myself I suggested that he play for a while. I went into the kitchen where I stood leaning against the bench trying to decide what to do. Suddenly I heard him begin to play. I recognised the music. One of the first that we had discovered together: Philip Glass's 'Mad Rush'. I sank down on one of the kitchen chairs and listened. He played slowly, slower than I had ever heard the piece played before. And after a while I realised he was improvising large sections. The pulse increased gradually and I was hypnotically pulled into the music. I had never heard him play like this before. In part, it was painful to listen to, but it was also breathtakingly beautiful. I closed my eyes and pinched the bridge of my nose to stave off my tears.

When the music stopped I went back into the room. Ika sat on the piano stool, slowly closing the lid. As he placed his hands on the closed lid and bent forwards I could see the dark bruises around his neck.

'Here is what I think we should do,' I said. 'I will call Mr Brendel. You remember him, don't you? The farmer who lives up the hill on the other side of the road?'

Ika nodded with his eyes on his hands.

'I will ask him to drive us to your home. I will come too, of course. And I'll talk to your grandmother. Then we'll decide what is the best thing to do.'

No response.

'Is that okay?' I asked.

He kept his head bowed, but after a moment he shrugged his

shoulders. I longed to hold him, find a way of comforting him and make him believe I could help him. And convince myself as well. All I could think of saying was: 'It will all come right. I promise you it will all come right.'

I listened to my own words. They sounded hollow and I didn't think they sounded comforting at all.

I went and rang George.

10.

I don't know what I expected. I had never really given any thought to Ika's family or homelife. To me he had seemed like a solitaire with no connection to anything or anyone. Stupidly, I had never asked. And he had never volunteered any information.

The small weatherboard house sat on a piece of flat land covered in yellowed grass. It looked abandoned; there were no signs of life. No washing on the clothesline that slowly turned in the breeze. No flowers. No curtains: the windows were black holes. The section was unfenced, marked only by a shallow ditch along the unsealed road and a low hedge of dead macrocarpa on one side. I could see no other houses and no animals, so perhaps fences were superfluous here. George drove up and parked on the dry yellow grass near the house, beside half a dozen car carcasses in varying stages of decay. Two large mongrel dogs came running towards the car, furiously barking. We stayed in the car with the doors closed, waiting.

The woman who eventually emerged through the open front door was small and very thin. From where I was I couldn't judge her age, but she walked with a slight limp, or perhaps with exaggerated caution, as if she were in pain. She called the dogs and they withdrew reluctantly, whimpering.

'How about you and I take a little drive? Leave the ladies to themselves for a little while?' George turned to Ika in the back seat.

Ika didn't reply, but made no effort to get out. I took this as a yes, as did George.

'Thank you,' I said to him and stepped out of the car. I really meant it. 'It shouldn't take very long.'

I had no idea how long it would take of course. Or what 'it' really encompassed. I just felt I had to say something that sounded – well, normal.

I watched them drive off, leaving a slowly dissolving cloud of dust behind. The woman stayed where she was just outside the front door in the shade of the jutting roof. She had crossed her arms over her chest. It was easy to see she wasn't looking forward to this. Nor was I.

I introduced myself but she didn't offer her name.

Instead she interrupted me impatiently. 'I know who you are.' She waved one hand dismissively.

Again, I felt the familiar pang of alienation. They knew me; I didn't know them. I wasn't one of them.

'Can I come in?' I asked.

She cocked her head and looked at me briefly, making it clear that I mustn't take it as a given. She waited just long enough and then looked me straight in the eye for a fleeting moment. She had strangely pale blue-green eyes, set off against her light brown skin. Then she turned and walked back inside. I hesitated for a moment before I followed.

The house had no smell, and this somehow surprised me. It was bare and dry, void of signs of human life. The hallway was dark and completely empty – there were no pieces of furniture, no mats, not even rubbish. No shoes by the doorway. Nothing. Just a clean, worn strip of linoleum running the length of the narrow space. I could hear a TV or a radio from behind one of the closed doors but there was no sign of any other person in the house and there were no other sounds. The TV playing for nobody seemed to emphasise the feeling of forlornness that filled me the moment we drove up outside.

I followed the woman into the kitchen. It was very basic: a bench with a sink and stove. A worn, scratched fridge. Everything looked utterly clean, but the very cleanliness of the house was disturbing. It was aggressive, and it had nothing to do with comfort or care. She nodded for me to sit down on the one chair at the table, and I did. She went and got another chair from the corner and sat down opposite me. She said nothing but took out a pouch of tobacco. She rolled herself a cigarette, which she lit.

As she turned towards the window to exhale smoke I could see her face properly for the first time. Probably about my age. Over fifty. Too old to be Ika's mother, most likely. She had a strong face with regular features and those striking light blue-green eyes, but whatever beauty might once have been there was long gone.

'I am here to talk about Mika,' I said. 'I found him in the sea yesterday.'

She inhaled heavily and released the smoke through the corner of her mouth. She made no comment.

'I think he was trying to kill himself,' I said, bending forwards across the table to emphasise my words. The Formica table was cool under my palms.

She closed her eyes, inhaled deeply and shook her head slowly. She still didn't speak.

'I have got to know Mika a little since we first met last year,' I continued. 'He comes to my house most weeks. On Thursdays. His choice. I don't know why Thursdays and I have never asked. But I appreciate his company very much and I am very fond of him.'

I paused briefly and she opened her eyes. She still said nothing.

'But he has never told me anything about his home. And I have never asked. Perhaps I should have.'

She looked at me, sucking at her upper lip. Her lower jaw was virtually toothless. Then she rose abruptly and walked up to the window. She stood with her back to me.

'I do what I can,' she said. 'It's hard.'

I waited for her to continue.

'There is something not right with him. Always was. No wonder, perhaps, considering. Might have been Lizzie's fault.' She paused for a moment. 'Well, not her fault exactly. But she was in a bad way when she had him. Could've been the drugs. I don't know. But there was something wrong with him. Everything was wrong.'

She sucked on the cigarette and smoke lifted above her head and found its way out through the mesh covering the open window. She turned around and looked at me. It felt like an appraisal, as if she were judging my ability to absorb what she was about to say. How I would react. Her face was a dark shadow against the window behind.

'It's not easy, you know. I can't be here all the time. I have a job in town. Then there are the twins, though I can't have them here right now. Not since Joe came back. Since the accident I've had to keep him here.'

Her tone of voice had changed. The words flowed more quickly, confidently. It felt as if what she was telling was practised. A prepared story – perhaps not for this purpose particularly but for more general use. And it was as if she were testing it on me. I felt distinctly uneasy.

'Joe is not right in the head either. And he never will be. He's twenty-three, but in his head he's more like three. A big, strong, dangerous three-year-old. Him, I'm stuck with forever.'

She coughed, a deep scratchy sound that shook her thin frame.

I tried to work out who Joe and Lizzie were. I assumed Lizzie was the woman's daughter and Joe her son. The twins must have been her younger children. And Mika her grandchild. Lizzie's son.

She stood up and went over to the sink where she stubbed out the cigarette. When she returned to the table and resumed her story the words were hesitant. Uncertain. She spoke quietly and kept her eyes on the table.

'Lizzie was my oldest,' she said, as if she had read my thoughts. 'Mika's mum, though all she ever did was give birth to him. And then she died. Obviously nobody had any idea who Mika's dad was. Considering the circumstances. And so I ended up stuck with him.'

She leaned backwards a little and looked at me with an odd expression. As if she were challenging me. Testing me. Then she carried on, more confident now.

'Joe is my only son. Not that he has ever brought me much joy. And then he drove himself off the road two years ago. The doctors thought he was going to die. That might have been better. But he didn't. Nothing but trouble before the accident, but there was nothing wrong with his head then.'

She looked up at me and for a moment I felt that she was letting me in. For a fraction of a second it felt as if I caught a glimpse of this woman's most private inner self. And as I looked at her across the table I thought I saw her in a different light.

'But you know now he's dangerous. I've had to face it. It's as if something has been destroyed inside him. Like what little control he had before is gone. I can't leave him alone with the other kids. Or with anybody, really. Sometimes I think it would be better if he was locked up. But they don't lock you up for being dangerous,' she said.

'You have to do it, don't you? Murder someone. Rape someone. Just thinking about it isn't enough.'

She stopped and looked down on her hands, which lay folded on the table. She stretched out her fingers and held on to the edge of the table for a moment. I noticed that the nails were coarse and long, yellowed on the right hand. The fingers were bony with swollen joints. Her hands looked hard.

'It's a terrible thing for a mother to say, I know. But I can't watch him all the time, can I?' She looked at me and her extraordinary eyes were wide open and very pale. 'And if I try the best I can, that's all anybody can ask, isn't it? I do what I can, the way I can. Teach him the only way I know.'

What did she mean? And who was 'he'? What did she expect me to say? Or do? I felt as if I were missing something. That there was an elusive aspect of her story that I couldn't catch.

She sat back a little and folded her arms across her chest.

'And if it's sometimes too much, who's to say? Eh?'

Abruptly, everything I had prepared in my head dissolved. The camera with the photos of Ika stayed in my handbag. I had only one goal. I had to take him with me.

My heart was thumping so hard I had trouble hearing what she was saying.

'I try to get the kid off to school before I go to work. But I can never be sure where he is off to. I don't know what's going on in his head. It's as if he's in his own world. I tell him to wait in town till I'm finished at work but he never does.'

She fingered the tobacco pouch on the table, but withdrew her hands and clasped them.

'How old do you think I am?' she said suddenly with a crooked smile.

I didn't know what to say.

'I'm forty-two.'

Again she looked straight at me with that strange expression, as if she were challenging me. But the effect was pale and weak, like a distant echo of a personality now almost lost.

'Yes, I know how I look,' she said and smiled a thin smile that failed to reach her eyes. 'But there is a guy I used to know. Joe's dad. Up north, he is now. He says he's willing to take me back. And he's willing to take Joe too. Says he can put him to work. Used to be a bit of a wild guy himself. Hard, you know. I have the scars – and pain – to prove it. But he's not a bad bloke really. I think he's settled down. And I think he can manage Joe. Says he'll let me have the twins come later, if things work out.'

She opened the pouch and rolled another cigarette.

'But he won't have Mika,' she said, peering at me as she exhaled smoke. 'Truth is, nobody can stand him. Nobody wants him. Nobody. Because there is something not right with him. Nobody wants broken things.'

I still couldn't think of anything to say.

'It might not work out, but God knows I'd like to give it a go. I've got nothing here. But if I go I can't take Mika. And then they'll take him into care. And who would take him? I mean, they have all these normal children to choose from. Who would want him? Where would he end up?'

She paused and the kitchen went awkwardly quiet.

'Plus I'd lose the benefit.'

Her eyes stared into space and she wiped her mouth with her hand. Then she turned to me and suddenly I could feel her despair. Sense the glimmer of hope of a future for herself fighting with the enormous burden of responsibility she had been dealt.

Then I heard myself speak.

'If you want to try it out I could consider having Mika stay with me.

Just for a while. Until you see how it goes. I mean, you may decide to come back. It would be more like a holiday. Just to see. And for now, we needn't involve the authorities. You can keep the benefit. Till we see how it works out.'

In the silence we sat looking at each other, both equally stunned, I think. It was not what I had come prepared to say. I could no longer remember what I had planned. And this wasn't what she had antici-pated either, I could tell.

The woman opposite me seemed to have straightened up on her seat. She cupped her right elbow in her left hand as she moved the cigarette and exhaled smoke in one swift, elegant move. Then she screwed up her eyes and looked at me with an expression of suspicion.

'Why?' she said finally.

'Why what?'

'Why would you do something like that?'

'Well,' I said, hesitating for a moment, 'like I said before, I have become fond of him. I live by myself not far from here. I only work occasionally, so I'm mostly at home. I am a . . .'

'I know where you live. And I know where you work,' she puffed her cigarette impatiently. 'But why would you want to take the kid?'

I struggled to find the words to explain to her what I couldn't quite understand myself.

'I like having him around. He is company for me. And I enjoy teaching him music.'

'What do you mean?' she asked. 'Those strange noises he makes?'

'I don't know what you mean by strange noises,' I said. 'He plays the piano when he is at my house. I believe he is gifted.'

Her laughter startled me. It was shrill and hard and it ended as abruptly as it had started.

'Piano?' she said incredulously.

'Yes,' I said. 'I think he is exceptionally musically gifted. He may need a better teacher than me soon, but for now I still have things to teach him.'

The awkward silence felt precarious. We were poised there; the scales could tip either way. It seemed that our thoughts had taken off in different directions – the moment of intimacy and understanding had passed. She kept looking at me with that expression of utter suspicion.

'It's only for as long as you want,' I said, bending forwards and resting my elbows on the table. 'And only if Mika agrees to come.'

As if on cue, I heard the car drive up and the dogs starting to bark.

We both rose at the same time and she walked ahead through the dark hallway. At the far end, and before calling the dogs, she turned to me.

'I'm Lola.' She held out her hand. 'If you wonder about the name, it's from a film my dad apparently liked. A German film about a whore, as far as I know. Sums him up.'

She held on to my hand and looked straight at me. The grip was uncomfortably hard, and held for too long. I was relieved when she finally nodded and let go.

George and Ika approached and we all went back inside. In the kitchen we stood in silence until George pulled out one of the chairs and gestured for Lola to sit, which she did without a word. He then pulled out the other one for me.

'I'll wait outside,' he said, and left.

I sat down.

Ika stood by the kitchen door, looking at neither of us.

'Come here,' Lola said, and Ika took a few steps forwards, stopping well out of reach.

'This woman says you can stay with her. I need to go away for a bit, see.' Her expression made it clear that she expected no reaction, and none came. Nothing indicated that he had even understood what she said.

I stood up and crouched in front of him, making sure to leave enough space between us.

'Ika, I have asked your grandmother if she would let you stay at my house while she is away. But it's for you to decide. Nobody will force you. It's entirely up to you.'

He said nothing.

'It would make me very happy if you came,' I added. 'We can play music. And I can take you to school in the morning and pick you up in the afternoon.'

It sounded like a plea. Who needed whom here?

Lola and I both looked at him. I assumed that she was as keen as I was to see some kind of reaction. But once again, nothing. Then he turned abruptly and left the kitchen.

I went back to the chair and sat down.

Lola sighed and shifted in her seat, as if she were uncomfortable, or in pain. She shrugged her shoulders and reached for the tobacco pouch.

'Well,' she said, 'I don't think we'll get much out of him.'

Suddenly I realised how much I had anticipated having him come to stay. In my thoughts I had already started planning things to do. Food to cook. Music that we would listen to, and music that we would play. Walks. At the same time I envisaged the process I would initiate if I decided to report the abuse. A process that would be entirely out of my control. And the concern for his welfare that would follow, the issue of whether he would remain with me, or be taken into care. My heart sank as I considered the alternatives.

Just as I was preparing to stand, Ika returned.

He was clutching a tattered shoebox under his arm.

'Are you coming with me?' I asked quietly.

He stood in the doorway holding the box, his head bowed.

Then he looked up and his eyes locked with mine for the briefest moment before setting on the usual point just beside my head. I could have imagined the bit about our eyes meeting. But there was no doubt about what he said.

'Yes.'

I wanted to lift him. Hug him. Put my hand on his head. But I checked my impulses.

Instead, I crouched slowly in front of him again.

'You have made me very happy,' I said.

He turned abruptly and left.

Lola stubbed out her cigarette in the sink. She smiled her crooked smile with closed lips. It wasn't really a smile. There was no joy in it and it made me feel ill at ease.

'That's as close to saying he likes you as he will ever come,' she said. 'I'll go and get his other stuff.'

I went outside and stood by the front door for a moment. Ika and George were standing by the car. George seemed to be talking and they were both looking intently at one of the wheels. I couldn't help smiling.

As we left I turned in my seat and looked at the small person in the doorway behind us. She stood immobile for a moment, then she disappeared inside.

We went over the small ditch and up onto the road. As the car picked up speed, George turned first to Ika in the back seat, then to me.

'That was a nice morning,' he said.

'What do you think, Ika?' I asked, looking straight through the windscreen.

'Yes,' Ika said.

I smiled again.

'It's been a very nice morning. A very nice morning indeed,' I said, and adjusted myself in the seat.

11.

George took us home. Afterwards, I realised I should have invited him in but as he dropped us off and we stood beside the car for a moment, all I could think to say was thank you. After a brief, awkward silence George promised Ika he would take him fishing on the Saturday. Then he waved and drove off.

I made tea and sandwiches and we sat down on the deck. It was early afternoon and the skies had cleared. We sat protected from the wind and it was warm in the sun. Ika had placed the shoebox on the chair beside him. I looked at it, wondering what it contained.

'Can I see what's in your box?' I asked. 'Or is it private?'

Ika said nothing, but picked up the box and put it on the table.

'Can I?' I said, and put my hand gently on the lid.

He nodded.

I lifted the lid. There wasn't much inside.

A worn toothbrush.

A tattered plastic bag containing what looked like a baby tooth.

A tattered photograph of a young dark-haired woman holding a small baby wrapped in a blanket. She wasn't looking at the baby but straight into the camera, with an expression that was hard to interpret. There was no joy there. She held the baby as if someone had passed her an unwanted parcel. She looked very young but her expression and demeanour suggested anything but youthful innocence. I presumed it was Lizzie holding her son in her arms.

A small knife with a rusted blade.

A fine filigree silver cross on a broken silver chain.

A small number of surprisingly beautiful seashells that didn't look like anything I had ever found on the beach. Nor did they look like those artificially polished ones you buy in tourist shops. I wondered where they came from.

And then, underneath all the other things, my little wind-chime made of paua shells. I had wondered where it had gone, and had assumed that the wind must have ripped it off its nail. But here it was, and again I felt that lump in my throat. What was happening to me?

I looked at Ika who had his mouth full and was staring past me and out to the sea. His face was expressionless. I had no way of knowing how he felt.

I took out the wind-chime.

'Let's find a good place for this. It likes to be in the wind, I think,' I said.

I held it out to Ika and he stretched out his hand. He walked over to the spot where it used to hang and reached up to hang it on the nail. As if on cue a waft of wind picked up the string of shells and they rattled cheerfully.

He turned and walked over to the hammock that hung from the

ceiling. He crawled into it, adjusting himself till he half sat, half lay. The hammock rocked gently. And then he lifted his eyes and looked at me for a moment. I made sure I kept my own eyes on the sea. He didn't smile, but to me it felt as if he did. He just briefly nodded and closed his eyes.

I leaned back in my seat and closed my eyes too.

Mother holds her hand, but it doesn't feel as if she is supporting her. It doesn't feel as if anything at all comes from Mother's hand. It is cool and dry and feels as if it is hardly touching her own. Every now and then the grip loosens, then tightens again, as if it needs to be reminded of what it is doing.

She holds her small tartan beauty box firmly in the other hand. It contains her most precious things. Mother is carrying her own suitcase. Marianne doesn't need one, because her few things are packed in Mother's suitcase. Mother has told her she will need new clothes once they get to Stockholm. City clothes. She wonders what they will look like, but it doesn't make her happy to think about them.

She is so very tired. She has been sick on the bus and there is a sour taste in her mouth. Her stomach feels like an empty hole, but she is not hungry. She just feels like crying.

They walk under a canopy of green leaves. There are double rows of tall trees on both sides of the pathway and the branches meet over their heads, keeping the sunlight out. It is cool here in the green shade, but she is still warm from the bus ride. Her skirt sticks to her thighs at the back and she tries to pull at her underwear without being noticed. She carries her doll under her arm, and the doll is dressed for travel too, in her finest flower-print dress with smocking on the chest, matching her own. Mother is trying to prevent her high heels from sinking into the gravel, and every now and then she loses her balance slightly. Then the grip on her hand tightens and it feels as if Marianne is the one supporting Mother.

'Not far now, Marianne,' Mother says and you can hear the smile in her voice. She doesn't want Mother to smile this new smile. She wants her to stop. She wants Mother to stop and crouch down and look her in the face. And she wants Mother to say that they don't have to do this. That they can turn around and catch the bus back. That she doesn't have to make this journey across the sea.

But this is not what Mother does.

'It will be exciting. Just wait!' she says instead. 'It is a grand ship, not like anything you have ever seen before. You won't even notice that you're on the sea, that's how big it is.'

And it is true, the part about the size. As they walk down the slope to the harbour she can see it. It really is bigger than anything she has seen before. Bigger than any house, even bigger than the church back home. When she was out with Grandfather in his little rowboat they would sometimes see large ships in the distance. But they had seemed like something that lived far away in another world. Silent, slow-moving bodies outlined against the horizon, as alien and as distant as the moon and the stars. Grandfather had showed her pictures from when he sailed around the world, but they were never pictures of the ship itself, just of tanned smiling men in a place that could be anywhere. She has never seen anything like this.

But it's not true that she doesn't notice that she is on the sea. As soon as they leave the harbour it is as if there is no longer anything to hold on to. The world has suddenly softened, lost its structure. Everything begins to feel uncertain, shifting. There is a strange feeling in her stomach, as if it is shrinking, until it is a burning ball. She takes short quick breaths, trying not to notice how it feels. But it is as if something is rising out of her burning hot stomach. It spreads and it grows, and it makes everything around her fade away. She sits absolutely still on the chair, holding on to her doll and taking the smallest gasps of air possible. If she moves at all, this horrible thing growing inside her will escape.

Mother is reading a book. She sits with her legs crossed and her wide skirt spreading over the seat, her foot with the red high-heeled shoe rhythmically kicking at the air. Marianne doesn't want to look but she can't help herself. She wants the foot to be still. She wants everything to be still. And she wants everything to disappear. And that is what seems to happen. Mother seems to withdraw, as do the rest of her surroundings, until she is absolutely alone in a white space where this thing inside her is the centre. She would like to ask her mother to help her, but it's impossible to speak while trying to hold back what is rising inside her. In fact she can't even shift the slightest on the seat. She looks at Mother, but she doesn't look up, doesn't seem to notice. It is filling her whole body now, this awful thing inside.

Then she can't hold back any longer. Violently it erupts, sprays over her dress and over the doll's dress too. She begins to cry, sobbing as her mouth fills with the foul vomit. She gags and it shoots up into her nose too. It hurts. Mother springs from her seat, brushing stains from her skirt. She is distant, still so very small. Mother looks around, as if she is hoping for help from somewhere. And it is forthcoming. A woman stops and they both bend down over her, but as another burst of vomit erupts from her mouth the woman retreats. They both take a few steps back. They will never be able to help her. Nobody can. She sobs and she weeps, she swallows burning bile that returns to her mouth instantly, only to trigger more burning retches. More vomit.

It is not until her stomach is empty and the retches find nothing more to expel, that they go to the bathroom to try to get her cleaned up. The smell of vomit follows them everywhere.

'Let's hope that's it, Marianne,' Mother says, trying to smile as she straightens Marianne's wet and wrinkled skirt. It feels cold against her skin. She is very cold now and her teeth chatter.

'We have a long journey ahead, Marianne. Perhaps you can sleep a little now. Let's go back and see if we can find a good seat.' Mother rises to wash her hands.

Marianne thinks about the long journey and she begins to cry again.

There is nothing to do about it. She will have to make this trip. Somehow, it must be possible. And somehow, she will have to learn to live over there.

They leave the bathroom, and it is only later, after they have disembarked in Stockholm, that she realises her doll has been left behind in the toilet. She doesn't tell her mother.

And now she doesn't cry.

12.

I opened my eyes and noticed immediately that Ika was no longer in the hammock. It swung empty in the light wind and I felt a moment's rush of panic. Where had he gone? Then I heard the music. He was inside, playing the piano. I listened for a moment and the flowing sound felt comforting. He wasn't going to run away. Not today. I had no way of knowing what he was thinking, but I knew that the only way for me to come to understand him a little was to give him time. Give us both time.

When I thought about my own memory of leaving home, the child's natural egocentricity struck me. I remembered only myself. My own despair. My utter loneliness, my grief. The overwhelming sense of hopelessness. And my total acceptance. But my mother was outside, distant.

Why had she suddenly decided to bring me into her life? I knew she was my mother of course. But the word mother had no meaning. I had no memory of missing her, longing for her. I had only seen her during brief visits at long intervals. She had never been a part of my life, nor had I been a part of hers. There was so little I knew. My grandfather rarely talked about my mother. When he did, it was just to give me little snippets of her present life, never anything about who she was. He would tell me she would be coming to visit the following week. That she had landed herself a new film role. That we should be proud of my beautiful mother. But it always felt so distant. As if she lived in another world that had no relevance to us or our lives in the village.

Instinctively I knew that it had been important to her, though. Claiming me and taking me with her to Stockholm seemed to be essential for her. And the look she gave Grandfather across the table as she took my hand was one of triumph. Much, much later, when I revisited my grandfather's village on one of the islands in the Åland archipelago, I stumbled across information that gave me some clues to Mother's need to prove herself as a mother. My mother. But by then it had no relevance. Or perhaps it did, in a way. Perhaps it was given to me to help me to find a place for my mother in my life's story.

Back then, as a miserable seasick six-year-old, I resigned myself to my new life, and I closed the door to what had been my life until then. I saw my grandfather only twice after that, and somehow his world had already slipped out of my grasp by then. Also, by then it was taking all my effort just to survive in my new environment. In my mother's world. I simply could not allow myself to hold on to the memories.

I wondered how this big step felt for Ika. I wanted him to understand that the door to *his* other world would remain open. That he was free to live in both worlds, on his own terms.

Besides, I had to accept that this was a temporary arrangement. I had no guarantee that I would be allowed to keep him with me. One day at a time, I thought. One day at a time.

The music stopped and I stood and cleared the table. It was time for our first proper walk together.

It was the day we started the project. The first day.

'I think you should make a big one. On the beach.' Ika was standing on the deck with his eyes on the sea.

'What do you mean?' I said.

'A big one like the ones you make inside.'

'An artwork?'

He nodded, but didn't turn.

'A really big one. So big you can only see it from above.'

What did he mean?

'But if I make it that big I can't see it while I am working on it,' I said. 'I won't know what I'm doing. Even with the ones I make here it's sometimes hard to see the whole thing and get the proportions right.'

'I can see it for you,' he said.

I wasn't sure what he meant, and I wasn't sure how to respond.

'Okay,' I said after a moment's silence. 'I'll try. If you help me.'

He said nothing.

'We'll need a lot of material,' I said.

'Yes,' he said. 'Let's go.'

And that was how we started.

I didn't quite understand what we were setting out to do, but the idea seemed to grow on me. We began to collect material and intuitively we picked more substantial things. Rocks that were so heavy I could only carry one at a time. Large pieces of driftwood. Feathers that we tied together into long ribbons. We created several stashes along the beach for the heavy material while we kept searching for the right location.

A couple of weeks later Ika asked me to follow him down to the beach. We walked further than we usually did, to a place where a small river forked before it reached the sea. The large stretch of sand between the two arms of the river was packed hard, and the surface was smooth.

'Here,' he said, his eyes on the space. I could see what he meant. It was perfect. Well out of reach of the high tide. It wouldn't be permanent of course, but here it would last a long time.

'Perfect,' I said. And Ika gave me one of his rare half-smiles, fleeting and without eye contact. It was almost as if he were mocking me. I had come to treasure those taunting little smiles, so quick that they were easy to miss.

'Let's mark it,' I said. There were some rocks further up the beach and I walked there and collected one. I placed it on one side of the flat surface of the sand. Ika shook his head and pointed a little further to the side.

'Here,' he said. I diligently moved the rock. We placed another three large rocks, one at each corner of the sandy canvas, and each time Ika directed me to the exact spot. When we were done he stood watching the space with his eyes screwed up. I stood beside him taking in the view too. And I was filled with a sense of excitement. Slowly, ideas began to take shape, and I could almost imagine what we were going to create.

'It will be wonderful,' I said, trying to control my urge to hug him. Ika nodded.

'Isn't it wonderful?' Mother says as she opens the door to the room. Marianne instinctively knows some response is required but she is so tired. So very tired.

'It is your own room, Marianne,' Mother says. But she already has a room in Grandfather's house, doesn't she? She doesn't want this big room

with its big bed and strange smell. But she doesn't want to cry, so she says nothing.

They have arrived in a taxi. There are houses everywhere – big houses so high you can't see the sky. Lots of cars, and lots of people. They live in a big house in Karlavägen. Number 63, on the fourth floor. They haven't walked up the stairs but have taken the elevator. She will have to remember all these things. But right now she is so tired.

When she has had a bath and changed her clothes, Mother takes her by the hand and leads her around the apartment. It is very big and the ceiling is very high. She doesn't want to be here alone, ever. When they stop by the window in the living room she can see cars moving along the street far below. She feels a pang in her stomach again.

'This is our TV, Marianne,' Mother says, and points to a box on a table in the corner of the small room beyond the living room. 'You will enjoy this.' Marianne doesn't understand what she means but she asks no questions.

Just then there are steps in the hallway and a man appears in the doorway.

He is old. He looks older than Grandfather, though he is very nicely dressed. He has no hair and the light from the chandelier reflects on the pale skin at the top of his head.

'Aha, this must be Marianne,' he says, looking down on her with his arms folded.

'Marianne, this is Hans,' her mother says. She pauses a little as if unsure how to continue. Then she says: 'My husband.'

Hans stretches out his hand but he doesn't move any closer. She has to walk up and take it. It is such a small hand, not at all like Grandfather's. It is soft and smooth and it holds her hand in a tight grip for too long. Because she doesn't know where to turn her gaze she stares at their joined hands. The nails on Hans's hand are long and they shine in the light from the lamp. It looks like a woman's hand, she thinks. She can smell his perfume. And when he finally bends forwards and opens his mouth she catches another strong, sweet smell. She would like to turn away but she can't do that. Her stomach tightens and she holds her breath.

'Let's hope we'll be very happy together,' he says. 'Anneli has been waiting for this for such a long time.' He looks at Mother and he's not smiling. Nor is Mother.

Later they have dinner in the kitchen.

'This calls for champagne!' Hans says, and opens a large bottle. The cork pops with a bang and hits the ceiling, where it leaves a small mark. Hans laughs.

They have strange food that she has never had before. Prawn cocktail, Hans says. Pale pink things that smell like fish, in a strange pink sauce. Her stomach knots and she holds back an urge to retch. She holds her fork and pokes around in the glass bowl, but she doesn't eat anything. Hans and Mother don't seem to notice. Now they smile and smile. And they drink from high delicate glasses – Hans more than Mother.

Mother has poured her an identical glass from another bottle. When she tries to balance the glass and take a sip, it seems to go straight up into her nose. She struggles to swallow and her eyes fill with tears. But they don't notice this either. Hans talks and Mother listens. She smiles and nods and her fingers play with a strand of hair. She looks very beautiful in the soft light.

'God, you're beautiful, Anneli,' says Hans and reaches for Mother's hand across the table. Mother smiles and lets him caress her hand where it lies flat on the table.

'Your looks. My talent and my contacts. Unbeatable. We'll go far,' Hans says. 'The world is at our feet!'

Then he turns to Marianne.

'Your mother will be world-famous, Marianne! Let's drink to that! Cheers!' And they raise their glasses, all three of them.

Later, Mother sits on Marianne's bed and strokes her hair.

'Sleep well, Marianne. I know it is all new and very different. But you will grow to like it. Life here in the city is so exciting. So much to do, so much to see.'

She looks at Mother's face. It feels as if it is burning behind her eyelids, but she doesn't know what to do, what to say. So she lies still and silent, on her back with her hands underneath the cold sheet. Mother runs her hand over the edge of the blanket but she doesn't bend down. Perhaps she doesn't know what to do either. They stay like this, in silence, for a long time.

'I have wanted this for so long, Marianne,' Mother says finally. 'It was just never possible before. Not till I met Hans.' Mother doesn't look at her, but towards the window. Somehow it feels as if Mother is talking to herself. Then she turns her head and looks down at Marianne. 'Hans is kind. You will come to love him.' She nods slowly, as if to make the words penetrate. Whether into Marianne or herself is not so easy to know.

'We will be like a family, Marianne.'

She says 'like' a family.

13.

It is strange how quickly we fall into routines. Begin to take things for granted. After a couple of weeks it was as if we had always lived together, Ika and I. And always would.

We organised a room of sorts for him. I cleared out the things I had stored in one of the wardrobes in the bedroom, and then we spent a day removing the back wall to make it open into the lounge. It was a deep space, intended to contain two double wardrobes opening from opposite sides, I think. Closing the door to my bedroom and opening it on the lounge side, it became like a little cave, just wide enough for a narrow bed and a chair. Before furnishing it, I asked Ika what colours he would like his room to be. He didn't reply straight away and I wasn't sure if he had understood.

'Come,' I said, and nodded for him to follow me into the kitchen.

From my piles of things on the bookshelf along the wall in the dining area I pulled out a colour chart I had picked up from the paint shop in town several months earlier. We sat down at the table and I pushed the chart over to him. He didn't seem excited, but then I had never really seen him excited. I was slowly trying to learn the subtle signs of emotion that he did demonstrate. Now, there were none that I could discern. He turned the pages slowly, seemingly without much interest.

Then, 'This,' he said suddenly, and pushed the leaflet back across the table.

He had picked a soft pale green, like the underside of olive leaves. For some reason his choice surprised me and sent a wave of emotion through my body.

'That is a lovely colour, Ika,' I said. 'It will make your room very beautiful.'

Next day after school we went to the paint shop and had the paint mixed for us. We also bought a bedspread a darker shade of green and a small striped mat. Ika insisted on holding the bags on his lap all the way back.

Painted and furnished, the small sleeping space looked very inviting. We hung a white sheet on a wire across the opening and I made a tieback from braided linen strips and showed Ika how he could use it to hold the curtain open.

He stood quietly looking at the result.

'Happy?' I asked.

He didn't respond. After a little while he went inside and pulled the curtain closed behind him. I heard him lie down and I went around to my bedroom where I tapped on the closed door of the former wardrobe. I waited. Eventually there was a soft tapping in response.

I smiled and went over to my bed.

Marianne's room is an alien world where she lives, but which never quite feels like her own. As time passes, everything becomes familiar in a way, but she never stops to consciously take in every detail. The smells. How the parquet feels under her bare feet. How the wide marble ledge along the window feels as she lets her hands run over it – smooth and cold at the same time. It never feels right to lie down on the pink bedspread. Not even to sit on it. When it has been folded back at night she slides into the bed that still feels foreign to her. She gets no comfort from it, no warmth. It is as if her body wants nothing to do with any of these things. It keeps holding back, and it feels as if she cannot breathe properly here. At Grandfather's she had never been conscious of the look or feel of anything in particular. She had been one with all that surrounded her there. But that world no longer exists. All she has now is this. Nothing here belongs to her, and she doesn't belong here.

Here in this quiet world there is no time. There is no next day. Just an endless now. She lives here now. But it still happens that she wakes up and for a second she has no idea where she is. Then a faint hope rises from deep inside her. And before she is able to stop it, she has a notion of something else. A memory of another place, another time. But this happens more and more seldom.

She slowly learns how to find her way around – in the apartment and in the nearby surroundings. Sundays they often walk to Djurgården: Mother, Hans and Marianne. The best days are the rainy ones, because then they might stop and visit the large museum that looks like a fairytale palace. There is one display in there that she likes the best. It has windows and you can look through them into different rooms, all with tables set for dinner. You can stand and watch with your head close to the glass and imagine the people who will eat there. The best room has a large beautiful table covered with a white tablecloth, and with candlesticks and vases with flowers. In the centre of the table there is a swan, its wings slightly opened, as if it has just landed. If she stands there quietly with her forehead resting against the glass she can sometimes imagine how happy they will be, the people who will soon sit down on the chairs and open the folded napkins. How they will talk and laugh while they eat their nice dinner.

They rarely have guests at home. Most evenings, Marianne has her dinner alone at the kitchen table, because Hans and Mother eat out, in a restaurant.

'Put on something nice, Anneli,' Hans calls out as he steps through the door such evenings.

Before they leave, Mother comes to say goodnight. Then she is beautifully dressed and her perfume is sweet and strong and drifts around the entire bedroom. Marianne can almost see it. Sometimes she reaches out to try and capture it in her hands, but when she puts her hands to her face she can smell nothing.

Some evenings Mother and Hans bring guests home with them when they return, but these guests don't come to eat. It is late, and Marianne has been in bed for hours, but she always wakes up when she hears the front door open. It sounds different when they bring guests. Happier. And she listens as they turn on the music, hears them talk, sing and laugh, and the glasses chink.

The girls come and go. The babysitters. Some often enough to become real people. Like Annette who lets her sit on the sofa in the living room and watch television until late. Annette wants to be a movie star and Hans has told her he will try to help her. If she looks at Annette and squints a little, Annette is almost as beautiful as Mother. But when she looks properly she can see that Annette's blonde hair is dark near the scalp, and her teeth are crooked. Annette says she needs to lose weight, but as soon as the front door has closed behind Mother and Hans she goes to the kitchen and opens the fridge to see what's there. Mother always puts out a bowl with nuts and sweets for Annette, but Annette still checks the fridge. And when she finds an opened bottle of wine in there she pours herself a glass. Marianne has to promise not to tell anybody. Then they sit together in front of the TV.

Marianne doesn't much like TV, but she likes to sit there with Annette and feel like a grown-up person.

One evening when Mother and Hans return, Mother comes into her room to whisper goodnight as usual. Marianne lies with her eyes closed. She can never be sure whether Mother thinks she is asleep, but it doesn't matter. This is what they always do. Mother tiptoes across the floor in her stockinged feet, and bends forwards and whispers goodnight. She never waits for an answer, but turns and leaves as quietly as she has entered, pulling the door closed behind her. But this evening she stops on the way out. She stands by the half-open door with her hand on the door-handle. It's dark in the bedroom but the hallway beyond is bathed in warm yellow light. Mother stands absolutely still just inside the bedroom door. It is strange. Why is she standing there? So still. Marianne cautiously shifts her head a little off the pillow, and she can see into the hallway. And there is Annette with her back against the front door and Hans very close to her. She can only see his back and a little of Annette. She can see how Hans tilts Annette's face upwards with his fingers under her chin, while his other hand pulls up her shirt a little and then slides inside. Then he bends forwards and it looks as if he is kissing her. All is very quiet and she can hear the sound of the cars driving past far below in the street.

Finally Mother moves, but instead of leaving the room she walks back to Marianne's bed and sits down. Marianne keeps her eyes closed and Mother says nothing. She just sits there. When Marianne eventually opens her eyes a little and peeks at Mother, she can see that Mother is looking towards the window, where snowflakes slowly and soundlessly dance in the darkness outside. She has taken out her hair clasp and is slowly running her fingers through her hair that falls over her shoulders. It is not until Marianne has to move her legs a little that Mother suddenly seems to come to. She turns her head and puts her hand on the blanket over Marianne's chest.

'Goodnight Marianne,' she says very softly, and the voice is not like *her usual one. Then she makes a little sound, like a quiet cough, and says a little louder: 'Goodnight, and sleep well.'*

This time she doesn't tiptoe, but walks across the floor with heavy steps, her heels pounding the parquet. When she reaches the door she seems to hesitate for a moment. There is the sound of the front door opening and closing. When the bedroom door finally opens, the yellow light flows into the bedroom and Mother is a silhouette. There is the sound of Hans's rapid steps along the hall. It feels like a very long time before Mother finally steps out into the hall and pulls the door closed behind her. It's as if she has taken the light with her and the room seems darker than before.

Annette never returns. And Marianne stops thinking of the girls as real people. They become like everything else here.

Foreign and fleeting.

14.

The very best part about my life with Ika was our joint project. To me, it felt as if for the first time in my life I was working together with another human being in an instinctive, almost telepathic way. I realised I had never experienced anything like this before. I had collaborated with other people both professionally and privately of course, but I had never felt that we were sharing the same task. Quite the opposite: we had divided the tasks between us. Not even in my marriage had I felt such a connection. My husband and I had lived beside each other, but I had had no insight into his world of ideas, nor he into mine. Never before had I experienced the joy of a truly joint project.

It felt as if I had been given a new life, or rather as if I were finally alive. I felt my cheeks blush from exertion as well as excitement, and each time we returned home after a day of labour I sat down filled with the kind of exhaustion that is good, and infinitely satisfying. I had no idea whether Ika was experiencing something similar.

We both had our assigned roles, and Ika was the project manager. But we did everything together. We needed each other. He had the plan in his head and he knew exactly where everything belonged. When we were out searching for material, he always knew exactly what he was looking for.

'Not that one, we need a bigger one. And darker,' he would say if I held up a rock. Or, 'We need more feathers. Grey ones.'

We had no stockpile; we collected our items one at a time, as we needed them. We never found something we liked and then created a spot for it. It was always the other way around. The plan took precedence, and then we searched until we found exactly the right item. Very early on I realised the plan inside Ika's head was complete and very detailed, and that it did not allow any impulsive adjustments.

We never noticed any interference with the installation: we always found it exactly as we had left it. And it weathered wind and rain without being damaged.

We didn't work every day. It took well over half an hour to get there, and some days there was not enough time. But as the days grew longer it became easier to spend time there after school. Weekends, we often brought a picnic lunch and stayed all day. We never invited anybody else, not even George. He probably wondered what we were doing – what was taking up so much of our time. But he never asked. And it didn't feel right to bring someone there before we had finished.

One day when we returned home later than usual, and sat at the kitchen table eating in semi-darkness, Ika suddenly looked at me across the table. Well, 'looked' might not be the right word, it was just the quickest little glimpse before he lowered his gaze again. Still, it surprised me.

'Have you ever had a child?' he asked.

I was completely unprepared for the question and I choked on my tea. Slowly, I put down the mug and tried to collect myself.

'No,' I said. 'I would have liked to, but it never happened.'

'Do you have a mum and dad?'

I shook my head.

'No, they died a long time ago.'

'A sister or a brother?'

Again, I shook my head. 'No,' I said, hesitating for a moment.

'I did have a brother, but I lost him,' I said eventually.

An extended pause followed.

'I can be your child. And your brother, if you like.'

His eyes were stubbornly fixed on his empty plate.

'Would you?' I said, and it turned into a whisper, because I could not quite trust my voice. 'You know, Ika, that would be the very best thing that could ever happen to me. The very, very best.'

He nodded.

And without another word, he picked up his plate and walked over, placing it in the sink. Then he left the kitchen.

I heard him brushing his teeth and walking into his small room.

After a while I got up, and went into my bedroom. I bent down and knocked softly on the partition wall that separated our rooms.

There was a quiet knock from the other side.

'I – never – wanted – a – fucking – child!'

The words come one at a time, almost in a whisper, yet they roar louder than anything she has ever heard before.

She is kneeling on the floor in front of the dollshouse. The parquet is cold against her shins and she shivers a little. She looks at the little people living in the house: a mother, a father, a little girl. And a baby. She has

92

turned on the light in the living room and placed the mother by the piano. The baby is in its crib in the children's room upstairs and the little girl is sitting on the floor near the piano. She hasn't quite decided where to put the father doll. She is holding him in her hand when she suddenly hears Hans's voice from the kitchen.

'Yours, that was fine. We had agreed that. But I NEVER wanted one of my own. NEVER! This will ruin everything.'

She has never heard him speak like that. Hans keeps saying things she doesn't want to hear. Even though he doesn't raise his voice, it feels as if he is shouting. She wants to cry, but this is so terrifying she is struggling just to breathe. She sits cold and stiff, and she can't make even the slightest move. The tips of her fingers tingle and when she looks down at her hands she realises she has broken the father doll in her clenched fist.

Mother is having a baby. Marianne knows because Mother has told her. The day before, Mother came into Marianne's room and sat down on her bed. She took up one of the cushions and hugged it to her chest.

'I'm going to have a baby, Marianne,' Mother said quietly without looking at her. Then she just sat there with the cushion in her arms and her neck bent. Neither of them said anything. But slowly, slowly Marianne felt something extraordinary happen. It was as if something light and warm began to spread inside her. There would no longer be just her. There would be one more. A sister. Or a brother. There would be two of them.

Smiling, she looked up at Mother and met her gaze. And her smile died, because Mother was crying. She was squeezing the cushion and she was moaning and rocking back and forth, as if she were in pain. Marianne could not understand. She could think of nothing to do or say. She stood beside the bed, waiting. Finally, Mother stretched out her hand and took hers.

'You will have to help me, Marianne,' she said. 'I don't know what to do.'

Marianne nodded. She was no longer smiling, but the warmth and light were still there inside her.

'I will help you, Mother,' she said. She sat down beside Mother, and

Mother's hand rested on her lap. She wanted Mother to feel the warmth, and she leaned closer and put her arms around her waist. They sat like that for a long time.

Now, as she sits on the floor, her ears alert even though she doesn't want to hear, she tries to hold on to that moment. And she finds it again. The warm light lives inside her and nothing can take it away. Not even those awful whispered words.

She hears the front door shut with a bang that reverberates through the rooms for a very long time. And now she is finally able to move again. She walks slowly into the hall. She stops at the kitchen door. Mother is sitting on a chair at the table, her face turned towards the window. It is midday but she is still wearing her pink dressing gown. Her hands lie flat on the table in front of her. The silence is terrible, and that silence belongs to Mother. Marianne is outside, watching.

She stands there for an eternity, her bare feet balancing on the wooden threshold.

Then Mother turns her head and looks at her. She can see that Mother has been crying again. There is a bright red blotch on her cheek, and she lifts her hand as if she wants to hide it, then she lets her hand drop back onto the table. They are as if frozen stiff; Mother on the chair, Marianne in the doorway.

Marianne takes a tentative first step and walks slowly across the floor. As she reaches the table Mother opens her arms and pulls her close. She presses her face into the soft pink material and she can smell Mother's perfume. Mother slowly puts her arms around Marianne and it feels as if they become one. Mother rests her chin on Marianne's head. She can feel tears falling into her hair.

'It will be a beautiful baby,' Marianne says quietly.

Mother doesn't respond, just keeps holding her tight.

'Yes, Marianne, it will be a beautiful baby,' she says after a very long time. 'And you will help me, won't you?'

Marianne presses herself hard against Mother's chest and she can feel her heart beating. She wants this moment to last a long time. She holds her breath and tries to be absolutely still. She knows that even the slightest movement, the softest sound, will end it.

Afterwards nothing will ever be the same. Everything has changed; it is as if something has suddenly pushed her closer to her mother. They are together, just the two of them, in this new world. Not by choice, but because they have to be. There is nothing else for either of them.

It is no longer just alien and lonely in the large apartment. Now it is dangerous, too.

Still, deep inside, she carries this new warmth.

A sister.

Or a brother.

15.

We slowly slipped into a comfortable rhythm, Ika and I. I picked him up every day from school, and most days we went to spend time on our project in the afternoon. When we were home, he either played the piano or was in his room listening to music. I had bought him a small portable player but he seemed to prefer my computer. I was happy because it meant we were listening, if not together, then at least at the same time. It felt as if we shared it.

His homework was a source of frustration. I met his teacher the week after he came to live with me. She had been nice enough but she was a little guarded and vague, as if she were reluctant to fully acknowledge her part in Ika's education. I was left with the impression that her overall reaction was relief that Ika was now not solely her responsibility. Ika, for his part, never expressed any feelings about school. As with food, he seemed to accept it with a kind of neutral lack of interest. He never demonstrated any wish to skip school, but nor did he express any enthusiasm at leaving in the morning. He never volunteered anything about his school days, and his responses to my questions were monosyllabic.

I soon discovered that he possessed streaks of ability. He was very good at drawing. Not figurative things, but geometric shapes. He could draw them with the correct perspectives and extraordinary detail. But they were never alive – there was no creative element involved. He also had an uncanny ability to learn things by heart. Some things. Things with rhythm. But also in this there was something lacking. It was as if he never took in the meaning. It was all about the rhythm.

He didn't seem to listen when I read him stories or pieces from the paper. I wasn't sure whether he could read in the proper sense of the word. He knew the letters of the alphabet, I knew that. But it was hard to tell whether he could absorb the messages contained in the words and sentences. He never asked me to read to him. It was only when one day I pulled out my old tattered storybook, the only belonging that remained from my early childhood, that something seemed to change.

After we had made a room for Ika out of my wardrobe I had been forced to go through my things and I had slowly worked my way through cupboards and drawers till I finally reached the bookshelves in the living room. I was on my knees on the floor and opened the worn book. I held it up to my face and took in the dry smell, let my palm run over the pages. The book had naturally opened at the beginning of my favourite story, 'Lasse i Rosengård'. Although Grandfather had started reading it to me when I was very young, he had made no attempt to avoid the frightening parts, or soften them. But he always held me on his lap when he read.

There I was on the floor, a middle-aged woman in a house on the other side of the earth, and all the feelings that were forever associated with the words that had been stashed away for so long washed over me. I read and I remembered. I remembered how the story had frightened me, but also how secure I had felt in Grandfather's arms. I hadn't noticed that Ika had entered the room, but I suddenly felt him standing nearby.

I looked up.

'I have kept this book since I was a little girl,' I said, and held it up with the cover facing Ika. 'My grandfather used to read it to me.'

In his usual fashion Ika said nothing, but walked over and sat down on the sofa.

'Would you like me to read a little to you?' I asked. He didn't respond, but he moved over as if to make room for me beside him. Not very close, but still on the sofa. I walked over and sat down at a mutually comfortable distance.

And so I began to read to him. Slowly, since I had to translate from Swedish as I went. He showed no impatience but sat absolutely still, almost without blinking. His face was expressionless, as usual. After a while I was too absorbed in the text to notice anything around me. When I eventually paused and looked up I could see that Ika sat with his arms around himself, rocking a little. I was overcome by an almost irresistible longing to pull him towards me and hold him in my arms.

'Would you like me to stop?' I asked instead. 'Is it scary?'

He didn't answer, but he shook his head. It was hard to know what he meant.

'Read,' he said finally.

And I continued.

'And Grandmother was right. Mrs Terror never left Lasse alone. Each time Lasse went through the forest she would be hiding behind a rock, or behind a tree trunk, waiting for him. He never quite caught sight of her, but he knew that she was there and that she could fall upon him at any moment. So what? you might say. Surely he could have asked her to make

herself scarce and leave him alone? Yes, one might think so, but Mrs Terror is no ordinary woman – she is one of the worst witches on earth. And she has made greater heroes than Lasse from Rosengården take flight.'

I finished and closed the book. Ika stretched out a hand and I gave it to him. He sat fingering the closed book for a moment, then opened it and began to flick through the pages. After that first reading, the story about Lasse became his favourite. He had me read it again and again, and he never seemed to tire of it. He always seemed to listen with his full attention. At first I tried to talk to him about the story, but I quickly realised he had no interest in this. He just wanted to hear me read it. So it was impossible to know how he interpreted the story. Whether it resonated with something in his own life. All I could do was keep reading it to him.

The weeks went by. A couple of months. I heard nothing from Lola. I had no idea where she was, but I knew there were new tenants in the house. Ika never asked about his grandmother. I suppose we both had our reasons for not discussing the situation. And eventually I began to believe we would be left in peace.

Ika seemed to make some improvements at school. Each time I talked to the teacher she sounded more friendly, warmer. He still showed no particular enthusiasm for school, and he still didn't talk about it voluntarily. His replies to my questions remained mono-syllabic. But I felt that things were improving. Or at least stabilising. At home, too. We had established comfortable routines. I thought that Ika was as contented as I was. I experienced moments when I was overcome by something that resembled happiness. It was as if we were slowly growing into an unusual little family.

Our project progressed. It was still hard for me to envision what it was that we were creating, but in a strange way it was as if Ika were my eyes. I had developed some intuitive understanding of the idea in his head, and my ability to place things in the right place seemed to improve day by day. It was as if I felt our project, rather than saw it.

I had lived almost my entire life with no responsibility for anybody other than myself. I had had no sleepless nights with worries over a loved one. Never dreaded a late-night call. So the shrill sound of the phone in the middle of the night didn't evoke any anxiety. If anything I was annoyed, assuming it must be a mistake. A wrong number.

But it was Lola.

It took me a while to recognise the voice. I kept the phone to my ear while I struggled to disentangle myself from the sheets and sit up.

'I need him back,' she said with no introduction.

I froze. My whole body instantly went cold and stiff. I struggled to draw my breath.

'Why?' I managed to say finally.

'I just do,' she said.

'But . . .' I started.

She cut me short. Said she needed him with her. That Child, Youth and Family had been in touch enquiring about his whereabouts. That she was at risk of losing the benefit. I asked her where she was but she didn't respond. She just kept repeating that she needed Ika back. She wanted him the following day.

'No,' I whispered. 'Don't do this to him. He has just started to settle in here. He is making progress at school. Please, Lola, don't do this. There must be some other solution.'

But she was adamant, and nothing I said seemed to reach her. She would come and get him the following day. And with that she hung up.

I sat with the phone in my hand, stunned.

I tried to call her mobile but got a message that it had been disconnected.

I suppose I should have realised this was likely to happen. Nothing had ever been properly arranged. I had purposely allowed not just myself, but also Ika, to develop a false sense of security. Day by day it had become easier to believe we were safe. That our arrangement had become permanent.

I sat on my bed and stared into the darkness.

Then I heard the piano. Ika was playing. I didn't recognise the music. It was peculiar, not like anything I had heard him play before. It was a simple tune and he played slowly. Slowly, but with clarity and intensity. It was painful to hear. But I sat and listened. I didn't weep, but I was filled with a sense of awful helplessness and utter distress over my inability to influence the course of events. And in their awfulness the feelings were only too familiar.

When he stopped playing, the house became eerily silent, as if there were no longer anybody living in it.

I walked slowly to the lounge.

Ika was sitting at the piano. The room lay in darkness and I could only just see him outlined against the pale moonlight that shone through the window behind him. I walked over and sat down beside him on the stool. He didn't move and for a brief moment our bodies brushed against each other. He didn't look at me.

'Did you hear the phone?' I asked. I kept my hands between my knees to make sure I would not try to hold him.

He nodded.

'It was your grandmother.'

He didn't respond.

'She said she would like to have you back.'

I searched frantically for the right words.

'Would you like to go back?'

He said nothing and I couldn't see his face. Then I saw the trails of tears glistening on his bare chest.

I clasped my hands hard and struggled to control my voice.

'I will think of something,' I said. 'I will think of something.' I nodded to myself. Tried to reassure myself as much as him that there was something I could do. 'Your grandmother has problems, but we will find another way of helping her solve them,' I said. 'We'll talk to her tomorrow. Don't worry, Ika. Nobody will take you away from here if you don't want to go.'

He slid off the stool. I stretched out one hand and tried to grasp his but he was already out of reach. He left the room without a sound. I heard him return to his little den and pull the curtain closed.

I remained on the stool for while. I felt numb, unable to move or think clearly. Think at all. For the first time in my adult life I was overcome by a longing for someone to help me. Eventually I walked over to the sofa, wrapped myself in a blanket and lay down. I stared into the darkness until it gradually began to dissolve.

And I realised the new day had begun.

She is no longer a little girl. It feels as if she has become someone completely different. She is almost nine years old and she is all alone. She will have to learn to live like this. She is not sure how, but it is absolutely necessary. There is no other way. It is easier now that she is no longer Marianne. Now that she no longer has anything to lose.

Nobody has asked her anything. They have all been so nice. They look nice. They say nice things. Yet they have taken everything from her. They look over her head – at each other, not at her. Whisper behind her back. Talk about her as if they know. But they don't know anything. And she can't tell them because she is not that girl any more. It is empty inside her and nothing hurts. She is all new and she has nothing to tell. And she is absolutely alone.

'It will be all right, you'll see. You will be with your uncle. And your brother will be with a kind family who will love him and care for him.'

But they know nothing. They don't know how Daniel likes his milk.

How he likes to be stroked at the nape of the neck before he goes to sleep. He will be so frightened, and so very lonely.

But she is not afraid at all. She doesn't mind being alone.

It feels easier now. The old Marianne was so sad. She was still hoping. Longing. This new Marianne has no hope. No, she knows there is nothing more they can take from her. Because she has nothing. And she knows nothing.

She is absolutely certain she has never seen him before. The woman with the short red hair stands by her side, a little too close, as if she wants to make it look as if they belong together. She says: 'This is your uncle, Marianne.' She doesn't want to belong with this woman so she takes a small step away from her. The woman places her hand on her shoulder. Perhaps she is afraid that she will slip away. Why would she? And where would she go?

There is nowhere for her to go. And there is nobody who can help her.

On the way here in the car the woman turned towards her with the same hopelessly kind expression as all the others. Cheerful, but so very sad.

'It will be nice to be with someone from your own family, won't it?' she said, and patted her hand on the seat between them. She leaned so close that she could smell Marianne's breath, so she turned away and looked out the window. Marianne didn't reply. What could she say?

Because this man is not her family. She has no family. This man is a stranger and he means nothing to her. And she thinks that it looks as if he is thinking the same. But here they are standing facing each other. And she feels a little sorry for him. She doesn't need anybody to feel sorry for her, and it doesn't look as if he does. He doesn't look at her properly, but at the woman, who smiles and smiles. As if she thinks this will help.

'This is little Marianne,' the woman says.

'That's no longer my name,' she says quietly. And then again once more, a little louder.

The woman smiles an uncertain little smile but she says nothing. They stand in silence.

When she looks up at the man she can't see anything she recognises. He doesn't look like anybody she has ever seen. Not like her mother. And not like her grandfather.

But the woman says he is her uncle. Mother's brother. If this is true, why has she never heard anything about him? Never seen a single photo? Perhaps it is all a lie, just to make her go along with what they have decided. Make it feel better. They don't know there is nothing that can make her feel any better.

Just then he looks down at her, and he puts his hand on her head for the first time. Very lightly, and without a word. And somehow she understands that this is all he is able to do. And it is enough. It will have to be enough.

His name is Karl-Göran, but it will take her a long time to find out. Everybody calls him KG. The woman calls him Mr Gustafsson. It feels strange to stand here in front of Mother's brother. Where has he been all these years? She can't remember Grandfather ever mentioning him. Nor Mother. Except for that one time, when Daniel was born. When Mother came home from the hospital with Daniel in her arms.

Mother walked into the kitchen and sat down on a chair. She looked up at Marianne where she was standing in the doorway, and beckoned her to come closer. Then she opened the blanket and they both looked at the little face inside.

But she doesn't want to think about that now. Doesn't want to know anything about any of that. She no longer knows how it felt. That warmth that filled Marianne completely, that she knows nothing about now. It is as if she has never felt it, never stuck her hand in there and felt the little fingers grasp one of hers. She has never been so happy that she almost had to cry. She can't possibly understand how it felt to be that happy, and then look up at Mother and see that she is crying. Not because she is happy, but for real. And then hear Mother begin to talk. Now, she doesn't have to know how hard it is to be so happy and so sad at the same time. She doesn't know anything.

'This is your brother Daniel, Marianne,' Mother said. That doesn't sound sad at all, does it? But when Mother said it, it sounded so sad that it swallowed all the happiness.

'Always remember that you have a brother. And help me look after him.'

The person she is now would never understand. She would never understand what it felt like when Mother took Marianne's hand and put it on Daniel's small chest. How his rapid heartbeat felt under her palm.

'Love him if you can, Marianne. And stay close to him. Keep him close to you. I didn't, and I think my life might have been different if I had. But I allowed my brother to disappear from my life. When my mother left and took him with her, I let him go. And in the end I had nobody.'

That was all. Never again would she mention her brother. And Marianne never asked. This is not easy to understand, perhaps, but there were no more moments like that. Marianne never gave him another thought. She didn't even know his name. Or where he was. Whether he was alive. She just stored the piece of information together with the wealth of other incomprehensible bits and pieces that never actively surfaced again. Her mother had a brother. Somehow he had disappeared.

The old Marianne only had time for her own brother.

But here he is, her uncle, right in front of her. There is nothing she can do about that. She can't make herself not see him.

She is supposed to go with him.

He doesn't bend down to give her a hug, or even take her hand. That's a relief. Nor does he smile. And that's good too, because there is certainly nothing to smile at. He lets his hand rest lightly on her head a second time, that is all.

Then they leave.

She cannot know then that she will learn to love this man. And understand that he loves her too, in his way. It will take time, like all things that are created from nothing. One day she will grieve for him when he dies. But here and now, she can't even understand that she will ever feel anything at all.

But she follows him. This new girl, who is no longer Marianne, walks beside the tall man whom she doesn't know at all. They don't talk. What could they talk about when they do not know each other? They are two strangers who have been pushed together by others. So they walk side by side in silence.

They are to fly to London, because that is where he lives. She has never flown before, and abruptly she can feel her stomach knot. What if she gets sick? Vomits all over herself and others? She can't tell him. She just can't. For the first time since she became this new girl she feels her eyes sting with tears. But she doesn't cry.

And flying is not like being in a car or on a ship. All goes well.

They still have nothing to tell each other. Or perhaps they have too much pent up inside, both of them. The kind of things that are impossible to share with a stranger. So they sit in silence during the entire trip.

KG has no wife but he has Brian, who is waiting at the airport when they arrive. Brian is nowhere near as tall as KG, and at first it looks as if he has no hair. But close up she can see that it's shaved, and so short that it is just a faint shadow. He waves when he spots them, and when she looks up at KG she can see that he is smiling. It's the first time she has seen him smile, and he looks very different. It's as if his face was frozen before, and has now thawed. When he catches her gaze his face goes stiff again. But his cheeks are pink. She thinks that perhaps he didn't mean for her to see that smile. So she discards it straight away. She can do things like that now. Rid herself of anything hard or uncomfortable. Lock it away.

'There's Brian,' KG says.

When they get through the gate Brian opens his arms as if he means to hug KG. Then it looks like he is not sure what to do, and in the end he puts one hand on KG's shoulder and the other gently on hers. He says something she doesn't understand. She can tell it's English, that's all.

'Brian says he hopes you feel welcome. He hopes you will be happy staying with . . .' She doesn't understand why KG looks so uncomfortable. Then he looks at Brian and slowly puts his own hand on top of Brian's, which is still resting on KG's shoulder. He smiles again, and everything feels a little easier.

'Brian and I both hope you will be happy here. With us.' Then he rests his hand on her head for a moment.

Brian squats in front of her so that they are facing each other, and stretches out his hand. He is smiling, but this is not a sad smile. This is a good smile. So she takes his outstretched hand. He pulls her towards him and lifts her up. Although she is almost nine years old, he lifts her in his arms. And she lets him. She doesn't hug him but she doesn't resist either. And when she looks at KG she can see that he looks happy. Relieved, it seems. As if Brian helps to make things easier for KG. She looks at them both and she can smell Brian's perfume.

This is when it gets hard. She is scared she will burst into tears here, right at the airport, among all these people. She fights the tears, and it is very hard but it feels right. It is right that it should be hard. This is her punishment. This is how it should be. For a brief moment she had forgotten. She had smelled Brian's perfume and looked at KG and she had felt a sting of longing. She had wanted to lean against Brian's chest and put her arms around his neck. Cry. But she mustn't do that. It's just not allowed. And when she tells herself this, then the tears go away. It's good not to be Marianne any more, because she doesn't have to feel anything. She doesn't need to be sad, and can't be happy either. It's easier. Nor can she tell anything, since she knows nothing, remembers nothing. So there is no need to worry. She will not cry. And she will never tell.

Nobody asked her to tell then, when she was Marianne and would have been able to. And it's too late now. She is someone else now and she knows nothing. And when it gets really difficult, when hard things happen, well, then that is her punishment. And this feels good. It will make her stronger.

107

There is no need to be scared. It is just as it should be. She knows with absolute certainty that she will never share that, the most awful thing, with anybody. Not with these two, however nice they are. And she decides not to talk at all for some time. Until she can speak in English. This will make it easier. It will be like starting something new. A different life. In English. It will be like having a wall between what was before and what is starting now, and nothing can seep through this wall. In English, she will be able to live here. With KG and Brian.

Brian drives. She can see his shaved head above the neck-rest, but from the back seat she can't see his face. Mostly he is looking straight ahead. He doesn't turn his head, but every now and then he points at something outside and says something which KG then tells her in Swedish. She says nothing.

Time goes very slowly. Or rather not at all. It is as if they are here in the car, and it might last forever. But this is a kind of punishment too, so it doesn't matter. The back seat is very wide and the soft leather has a strange smell. The backs of her legs stick to it and she feels a little queasy. Not as if she needs to vomit, just a little queasy.

The woman in Stockholm tried to tell her how things would be. But what did she know? And what did it matter? The doctors wanted to know what she was thinking. But she had no thoughts because she was dead. She was nothing. They asked her if she was anxious and afraid. They knew nothing, all those doctors. How could she be anxious and afraid? Why would she be, when the most awful thing had already happened? She wasn't at all afraid. She was nobody, felt nothing, because it was all over. With their kind, sad smiles they sat watching her, their heads a little cocked, as if they expected something from her. Didn't they understand she had nothing to give them?

When they told her she was to move to live with her uncle in London she had no questions. It meant nothing. She would do as they said; it made no difference whatsoever. They could send her anywhere, ask her to do anything. She had no will. She had no wishes. She wanted nothing.

For they had taken Daniel from her.

It was her punishment; she was certain of that now. And she deserved it. What she had done was too awful ever to be mentioned.

That was why nobody had asked the right questions. Not even when they had just found them. Daniel and Marianne.

Mrs Andersson first.

Marianne had been there in the cot holding Daniel tightly. She could hear Mrs Andersson screaming. Running out into the stairwell and knocking on the neighbours' doors. Hear the doors banging and people running in and out. All the while she stayed where she was.

Even later, when Mrs Andersson crouched down and reached through the bars and stroked Marianne's hair, she burrowed her head in Daniel's back and refused to look up. She didn't want to see the look on Mrs Andersson's face. She could hear her sobbing. Mrs Andersson was weeping and it was the saddest sound Marianne had ever heard. Because Mrs Andersson should not cry, not her. It was horrible to have to listen to her weeping. When Daniel stirred, Mrs Andersson stood and bent down over the cot. She stretched out her arms and gently loosened Marianne's. Then she lifted Daniel and left the room with him in her arms.

It made no difference that Marianne screamed and screamed. When Mrs Andersson came back Daniel was gone. Mrs Andersson lifted Marianne out of the cot and carried her to the chair by the window. She sat down with Marianne in her arms and she gently rocked her. She didn't speak, but she hummed and hushed quietly. Marianne huddled up till she was very small. A very small child. She wept into Mrs Andersson's chest. And Mrs Andersson wept too.

But it didn't help of course. There was no help to be had.

Later, when they came to collect her, all those people with their sad little smiles, then she wept no longer. Then she stopped speaking too, because that didn't help either. They had taken Daniel, and nothing could change that. She cried when they took her nightgown, because it had a little of Daniel. Then she had no more tears.

She had nothing. There was nothing left. Not even Marianne herself.

And since nobody talked about that night, it felt as if it kept grow-ing, getting bigger every day. In the end it was all there was. It covered everything and made it impossible to see anything else properly. Made it impossible to feel anything. Whatever she saw, whatever she heard, it came through that night. Everything around her felt distant and unimportant. At first she had hoped that someone would ask the right questions. That she would be allowed to tell. She had hoped it in the same way a drowning person hopes. That someone would see her. Pick her up. Understand. And help her to understand. Help her to learn to breathe again. But nobody asked anything. They just smiled, their heads cocked. They patted her head. Promised her that everything would be all right. But how could it be? The only question they asked was how she felt inside. But that was the wrong question. That question had no answer.

They promised her that all would be fine. That is what people do when they know it is impossible.

In the end she came to think that perhaps they just didn't want to know. That what she had done was so awful that they could not bring themselves to talk about it. That what she carried inside her was as disgusting as vomit. It was understandable that nobody wanted to go anywhere near it. No, it was hers, all hers, and she had to keep it inside her. Nobody ever said a word about that which filled her completely. Then, when she was still Marianne, it was all that was inside her. Day and night. In her dreams. All the time. But around her there was only silence. They all looked away. And when they looked at her, they smiled, though there was nothing that would make anybody smile. There was no hope, she realised that.

Later, when she was no longer Marianne, it was as if she had drowned and returned empty.

Nobody ever told her where Daniel had gone. Everything would be fine, they said, but how could it be? When she no longer had Daniel? When he no longer had Marianne? How could anything ever be fine again?

She has no questions now. For she doesn't care. She wants to know nothing.

She looks out the car window, but all she can see are glimpses of roofs and treetops between pillars of grey concrete. She feels really sick: there is something inside that wants out. For the rest of the trip all she can do is try to hold it back. But eventually she falls asleep.

She wakes up to find Brian carrying her up the front steps of a white house.

'Marianne,' he says softly. And she knows that she has come home. But when Brian says her name it doesn't sound like Marianne. It sounds different and new. It sounds like Marion. She listens to it and she likes it, embraces it. 'Marianne' she locks up deep inside. And now it feels better, as if she has been allowed to take off something that has been hurting and chafing for a long time. She thinks that perhaps she will be able to live here, somehow. One day at a time. In English, being Marion. And Marion cautiously puts one arm around Brian's neck while they walk up the front steps of the large white building.

It is not until late that evening, when she is lying in a strange bed listening to unfamiliar sounds that she turns onto her stomach, buries her head in the pillow and finally cries.

For her brother. And for herself. For Marianne.

But it was chronological order I was after. I realised that even half-asleep my mind kept making its selections. Skipping the most difficult pictures. As if even now they were too hard.

The morning was bright and clear. The light flooded the room with a harshness that exposed everything.

I had to face the day.

16.

I knew he was not in the house. Had I willed him to run away? Or was it my impotence that had forced him to?

It was just after six. As I stood in the kitchen waiting for the kettle to boil I looked out the window. The wind was blustery, and light clouds stretched across the sky like cotton gauze. The sea looked grey and impenetrable in the early morning light.

I sipped the scalding tea and kept my eyes on the view.

I had no idea what to do.

I opened the door and went out to sit on the deck. Seagulls were squawking high above. They glided casually across the sky but the sound was piercing and shrill, as if calling attention to imminent disaster.

I went back inside. And then I called George.

He answered almost immediately, and I stopped short before I had even started. I stammered a few incoherent sentences before he quickly stopped me.

'Come over here, it is easier to talk face to face,' he said.

When I drove up to his house a few minutes later he was waiting on the front steps. On the way I had realised how early it was and as I stepped out of the car and walked up to him I watched for signs that he was annoyed at having been woken. But all I noticed was that his hair was wet, and that he had missed a button on his shirt. He smiled briefly and stepped aside, gesturing for me to come inside.

His house was nothing like what I had expected. I supposed I must have had some kind of idea of it, since it surprised me a little. It somehow felt as if it didn't belong in its surroundings. The house took me aback, yet at the same time it felt familiar. Cosy and somehow comforting. As if I had stepped into another, safer world.

I followed George into the kitchen and sat down on the chair he pulled out for me. I accepted a cup of coffee and watched his back as he prepared it. He moved without hurry, confidently and precisely. The coffee was strong and very good.

I searched for the words to tell him why I was there, but I realised I didn't quite know myself. I didn't know why I was there, nor what I expected him to be able to do.

In the end he spoke first.

'Let's take it one step at a time,' he said. 'You told me he has run away.'

I nodded.

'Yes, he overheard his grandmother ring last night. And I know it upset him terribly. He cried. I have never seen him cry before. I promised him I would find a way to prevent her taking him back. I said I would think of something.'

I looked at him, and for the first I time I noticed what he looked like. Until then he had been just a concept. My neighbour George, inseparable from the car he drove, the house he lived in, the land he owned. But here in the bleak morning light the individual features of his face suddenly became clearly visible. Brown eyes with a narrow yellow rim around the pupil. A long, arched nose. A wide brow with distinct horizontal wrinkles. Short grey hair, thinning on top. The hands on the table in front of him were large, but they didn't look like a farmer's hands. The fingers were long and the nails well kept, shining white against the darker skin.

'But when you don't believe your own words they don't sound very convincing, do they? I simply have no idea what to do. And Lola is expecting to pick him up today.'

George clasped his hands and looked down at them for a moment.

'I don't think you need to worry about the boy for now,' he said slowly.

When he looked up at me he didn't quite smile, but it felt as if he did.

'You understand what I mean, don't you?'

I nodded. Ika was safe. George knew where he was.

'I thought it would be best that you just know that he is safe,' he said, and I nodded again. 'If she appears today, it might be good that you don't know where he is.'

I understood what he was thinking, and I was moved by his consideration.

'It is the long-term solution we need to look at,' he continued. 'You really need to contact Child, Youth and Family.'

I nodded again, because he was only saying what I already knew. What I had known all along.

'Let me make a phone call and see if I can help you set up a meeting.'

It was not yet seven o'clock and I was surprised when he walked over to the kitchen counter where his mobile was charging. He grabbed it and left the kitchen as he punched in a number. I could hear him talking in the adjoining room but I could not discern the words. It took a while and I looked around the generous kitchen. It was well equipped and cosy. Not a bachelor's kitchen. It wasn't new, but everything was in good condition and it gave the impression of being solid and well kept. It looked lived in. Abruptly, I realised how bare and neglected my own kitchen was.

Then George returned.

He sat down and put the phone on the table.

'You have a meeting tomorrow morning. In Hamilton, at the CYF regional office. I'll write it down for you,' he says. 'You will meet the regional director.'

'Amazing that it could be arranged so quickly,' I said. 'And this early in the morning – it's not even seven o'clock.'

To my utter surprise he blushed.

'Well,' he said, hesitating a little. Then he cleared his throat. 'The regional director is a . . . an acquaintance. From way back.'

'Still, amazing,' I said. 'I am so grateful.'

'I assume you know this won't be an easy process,' he said. 'It will be hard to prevent the grandmother from taking him back if that is what she wants. Even if she loses custody it will be a long process, and an uncertain end result.'

'I realise that,' I said. 'And I realise I should have done this differently from the start. Made a report right then. But I just couldn't let him stay there another day.'

'We'll take it one step at a time,' George said and stood up. He collected a pad and a pen and scribbled down the details for the next day's meeting.

'Like I said, there is no need to worry about Ika for now,' he said as he gave me the note.

For a moment we stood facing each other.

'What time is she coming?' he asked.

'No idea. She didn't give a time and I have no way of reaching her. The mobile number she gave me when we met no longer works.'

'Just let me know if you need me. I will be here all day. Just a few minutes away.'

'Thank you. For everything.' And as I said this I was overcome by an overwhelming tiredness. As if I had finally allowed myself to acknowledge how exhausted I was. And I realised he had said 'we'. *We* will have to take it one step at a time.

I held out my hand and repeated my thank you. George took my hand in his and put the other one on my arm.

With this we parted.

Back home, my own house felt even emptier, as if completely abandoned. As if nobody really lived there. And I saw it more clearly than ever before. I could see how shabby it was. How worn and tattered. Filled with objects that sat or stood where they had happened to end up. Suddenly I was able to distance myself from it, as if it had nothing to do with me. I could see it objectively. I realised I had never made any effort to create a beautiful or welcoming home there. It was just a place to sleep, and it had a distinct desolate feel. It lacked any sense of homeliness.

The insight made me strangely sad. How could I not have seen this before? I had lived here for more than fifteen years. How could it be that it was not until now that I actually *saw* what it looked like?

It is strange how even the most extraordinary conditions can become everyday. You learn to live with pain, for example. That which initially seems intolerable becomes the only reality you have. And you adjust. You forget how it used to feel.

This was not a home, it was a refuge. This simple, desolate house had become the place where I had slowly learnt to live with my pain. The only place where the pain had been manageable, and where the memories didn't intrude. I was able to manage them here. This house had no connection with any other part of my life. And I had brought nothing with me.

The location was a different story. I had chosen it precisely because it was heavily pregnant with memories. But they were special memories. The most precious ones. The house itself was neutral. It demanded nothing, and it allowed me to nurture my memories in peace. For a long time this had been necessary for my survival. The house was my snail's shell. A part of myself.

I could no longer remember whether I had ever had any plans or ideas for the house. I had simply crawled into my shell in order to survive. I don't think I had any idea of the timeframe initially. I was driven by an acute, desperate need.

And the years went by. Perhaps at the back of my mind I thought it was a temporary arrangement. Until I could face the world again. Or perhaps I had thought of it as permanent in the beginning, and life without it impossible. Regardless, what had been created in a state of desperation had become permanent. The isolation itself had been a guarantee that nothing would ever rock my existence again. That I would be left in peace in the fragile stability it had taken me so long to establish. As it is with matters that you leave for later, I had simply become used to it as it was. Unfinished and neglected. I left it as I had first found it, and stopped caring.

I had not thought I would ever have reason to see it through somebody else's eyes.

But here I was, at the kitchen table, anxiously awaiting the arrival of an unwelcome visitor.

Later I went into the living room, turned some music on low and lay down on the sofa.

Marianne lives in a new reality. She is still in the same place, but everything has changed. She has started school. But it is not with happy anticipation that she sets out every morning, but with anxiety and a tight cramp around her heart. The school is not far away and she walks by herself. But it feels as if something is pulling her back, doesn't want her to leave. She has to struggle to make the short walk every day. But returning home in the afternoon she runs as fast as she can, and she exits the elevator breathless. She listens at the door while she is groping for the key chain underneath her jacket.

She has her own key, because Mother is so often tired. She has a woman who comes to help every day. Mrs Andersson. Marianne hardly ever meets her, because she is there in the morning, never in the afternoon. In the afternoon Marianne is there.

When she gets inside she drops her school bag on the floor, kicks off her shoes and runs into the nursery. And each time she sits down on the floor and spies between the wooden bars, she is filled with the familiar warmth. She feels all soft inside and finally the cramp in her heart lets go. All is as it should be. If Daniel is asleep she gently reaches inside and places her hand on his stomach. Then she pulls it back and puts it against her nose and inhales his smell. Often she lies down on the mat beside the cot and closes her eyes till she hears him stir.

Sometimes Daniel is already awake when she arrives, standing up in his cot holding on to the railing. When she steps through the door he smiles and bends his knees as if trying to jump, and rocks his body with a wide grin on his face. This means he wants to get out. And Marianne is allowed to lift him now. It's not easy but she manages because Daniel clings to her so tightly.

Then they play on the floor forever. Daniel can't walk but he can crawl, and he can stand up if he holds on to something. When he gets hungry she makes him a bottle and holds him on her lap while he drinks. If he is wet she changes his nappy. They manage very well on their own. They need nobody.

In the end Mother always turns up though. She moves slowly, and it looks as if she is not quite sure where she is heading. She never wears her nice dresses any more. Often she wears her old dressing gown well into the evening. When she spots Marianne she stops in the doorway and looks at her. She is holding her arms tightly around her chest as if she is cold. She looks at Marianne and smiles her sad smile. Then she nods slowly, before turning away and leaving. Marianne hugs Daniel even harder, sticking her nose in the space between his chin and his shoulder and inhaling the smell of him. In these moments everything feels all right.

One day she can hear Daniel crying inside as she pulls out her key. She tries to hurry and the key slips between her eager fingers. When she finally manages to fit it into the lock and can open the door she runs down the hall towards the nursery. But the crying hasn't come from the nursery. She turns the other way and runs to the living room.

There they are, Daniel and Mother, on the floor by the fireplace. Mother is holding Daniel on her lap. No, she is not holding him – he is just lying on his front across her outstretched legs. His cry sounds more like a whimper now, as if he has been crying for a very long time. And Mother is crying too.

There is blood on Daniel's singlet, and on Mother's dressing gown.

'I only left him for a minute,' Mother sobs. 'Just a minute.'

Marianne drops to her knees. She lifts Daniel and holds him. His face is all wet and he sobs and hiccups into her chest.

'He was on the floor . . .' Mother says, looking at Marianne. 'I just went to the bathroom.' She opens her arms and it looks as if she would like Marianne to hug her.

But now Marianne is crying too, and holding on to Daniel as tightly as she can.

'He fell on the poker-holder by the fireplace. And he cut himself.'

Mother lets her arms fall and wipes her nose with the back of her hand.

Marianne closes her eyes. She can't look at Mother.

'I did put away the pokers so he wouldn't hurt himself,' Mother says,

'but the holder was so heavy. I didn't think it could do any harm.'

Marianne gently sets Daniel down on the floor, stands, and then lifts him up into her arms. As she turns to leave, Mother slowly falls over on her side with her hands between her knees and she weeps even louder. Marianne crosses the floor with Daniel in her arms.

She goes to the nursery and puts him in the cot. Then she climbs in too. She lies down behind Daniel and now she can see the cut. It is an open gash, running from the base of the shoulderblade to the armpit. Blood is still oozing from it. But Daniel has quietened. The odd hiccup rocks him now and then.

Slowly, Marianne bends forwards and puts her lips on the wound. She sticks out her tongue and begins to lick. Her mouth tastes of salt and metal. Daniel falls asleep almost immediately. His pants are wet but the smell is warm and comforting. She pulls the blanket over them both and keeps licking the wound until it is clean and no more blood comes through.

Then she falls asleep, too.

The wound heals but it leaves a half-moon-shaped pink scar. Every night when they are in bed Marianne lets her fingers run over it.

It is even harder to leave for school now that Daniel is big enough to move around the apartment on his own. There are dangers lurking everywhere. New kinds of danger.

Sometimes Hans comes home before they are asleep. He bangs the front door shut and stamps along the hall. He never enters the nursery. Usually he goes straight to the living room and pours himself a drink. Then he turns on the TV. And often he goes out again later.

They don't have guests any more. And Mother almost never leaves the apartment.

Hans never tells Mother that she is beautiful. He says she is fucking ugly.

'Pull yourself together, for fuck's sake,' he says.

Mother says nothing. She doesn't cry. She just slowly walks away. Sometimes you wonder if she really hears what Hans is saying, or if she is really awake. Her eyes are open but it doesn't seem as if she is actually seeing anything.

Most evenings they are asleep when Hans comes home. He bangs and stomps even harder then, or that's how it feels. Marianne never knows when he will come. Sometimes he doesn't come home at all. But you never know, so Marianne sleeps with her ears open. It works. She opens her eyes the instant she hears the elevator. When it is late at night you just know it is him. The elevator door clatters and slams as it is opened, then closed. Then the front door opens with a bang. Hans stumbles and swears. Sometimes he slips and falls. Once or twice he has vomited in the hall. But it doesn't matter. Not as long as it happens out there in the hall. Or in the living room. But you can never be sure where he will go or what will happen. So you have to be alert.

Usually it is all right. Everything goes quiet eventually. But sometimes Hans goes into the bedroom and wakes up Mother. Marianne doesn't want to hear the things he shouts at Mother. And she doesn't want to hear the sounds Mother makes. She doesn't want to hear any of that. So she pulls the blanket over her head and puts her hands over her ears. Sometimes it is a very long time before it is finally over. When all is quiet Marianne can finally lift the blanket from her face. Then she is sweaty and needs to pee. But she doesn't get out of bed. The silence is too important. You mustn't disturb it.

But if she hears even the slightest sound from the nursery, well, then she jumps out of bed and tiptoes there as quickly as she can. She knows how to comfort Daniel when he has bad dreams. She climbs into the cot and lies down, closely pressed against him. She holds him tightly and puts a finger in his mouth. Then he stretches out his hand and gently plays with her hair until he falls back asleep. Marianne stays, sometimes until morning.

But then things change. It is as if a new time has started. A worse time.

When Hans is at home it is almost never quiet any more. Sometimes the police come because the neighbours complain about the noise. The police always leave again after Mother and Hans have talked to them. They never talk to Marianne.

Late one evening Hans shouts so loudly it echoes right through the whole apartment, perhaps the whole building.

'You fucking whore!' he shouts. 'You've ruined everything!'

Marianne has heard this many times before. But then he says, not at all loudly, but very slowly, with a pause between each word: 'I. Will. Kill. You.'

Then it is silent for a moment.

Marianne holds Daniel hard against her and his warm body is all that she can smell.

And then, not loud at all, yet even more terrifying, 'I will kill you both, you and the bloody bastard.'

After that there is no more sound. It is so quiet it feels as if the whole world has come to a stop.

From then on Marianne sleeps in the nursery every night. She waits till she knows Mother has gone to bed. This is always late, for most evenings Mother sits in the kitchen. She doesn't do anything, she just sits there. Sometimes she forgets to turn the light on when it gets dark. But eventually she goes to bed and Marianne tiptoes into the nursery and climbs into the cot.

Sometimes she wakes up because one of her legs gets stuck between the bars. Sometimes because Daniel moves. But she never forgets to keep her ears open. Even when she naps.

She is tired at school.

But school means nothing. She doesn't belong there.

It is here, at home, that she is needed.

17.

When I woke it took me a moment to realise where I was. But as I looked at the light outside the window I quickly realised it was still early morning. When I stopped working on a regular basis it had been as if dates, days of the week and even which year it was had become irrelevant. I no longer had much that required me to keep track of time. It was not until Ika came to live with me that I started using my watch again. Before, I had had days when I could allow myself to be guided by daylight only. I became good at sensing the time of day by just a quick look at the sky. Now, when I checked my watch I saw that I had been dozing for less than an hour. I felt stiff and sore when I stood up – my body reflected my state of mind. Slow and disjointed.

It might be hours before Lola turned up, and I had to stay in the house.

I felt restless, but there was nothing to do but wait. I fetched my book from my bedside table, but it was one that had failed to attract my full attention earlier, and did so even more now. I sat down at my computer and checked my email. A quick process – my correspondence was minimal. For the sake of something to do, I decided to write down what I needed to tell the person I was meeting the following day. Very soon the work absorbed me completely. I remembered incidents I hadn't given a thought to for a long time. The very first lunches. The early beach walks. The start of our project. When Ika had allowed me to plaster a cut in his foot, touch him for the very first time. I wrote it all down. Then I went to find my camera.

The pictures were awful. Worse here on the big screen. In close-up he looked dead. His eyes were closed, his face void of expression. It was like watching a body on an autopsy slab. I was unable to stop my tears.

I added the pictures to my text and printed the document. Scanned a letter from Ika's teacher telling me about his promising advances at school and pasted that into the document too.

As I was finishing assembling the papers from the printer I heard a car drive up. I froze and my heart skipped a beat. I dropped what I was doing and ran out onto the deck.

But it wasn't Lola, it was George.

'I've just come to see how it's going,' he said as he appeared around the corner. 'Have you heard from Lola?'

I shook my head and invited him in but he sat down in one of the rattan chairs on the deck. I offered him tea or coffee. Or lunch – it was lunchtime, I realised. He accepted and I went to the kitchen to see what I had to offer. Not much. My fridge only held some leftovers of the soup and a piece of cheese, and I had some stale bread. I heated the soup, just enough for two servings, and toasted the bread, and carried it all outside.

I saw that George was holding one of Ika's shells in his hands. At least it looked like one of them. He was fingering it and looking at it intently. I put the tray down on the table and he looked up.

'He gave me this. As if he wanted to pay me,' he said. 'At first I wasn't sure if I should accept it, but then I felt that was the best thing to do. That perhaps it would help to make him trust me. Make our agreement into a proper binding business arrangement.'

I served the soup and toast and poured tea.

The wind had died down and the sun was no longer directly overhead. The slightly oblique light enhanced the colours and created shades that gave new depth to all shapes. Suddenly the beach was no longer a flat stretch, but an undulating canvas of all shades of brown and grey, with soft hollows and rises.

'She might not come, you know. But that doesn't solve the problem, does it?' He looked at me.

'You can't just let it be. It needs to be resolved once and for all.'

I looked at him and nodded.

'It's hard to understand now how I could have been so stupid. So . . . Well, I should have known better, shouldn't I? After all, I'm a doctor. I know what to do in these situations. I *knew*. Of course I did. And yet . . .'

'But we're only human, Marion. Sometimes we do what our heart tells us. And sometimes that is the right thing to do, but sometimes it's not. Our emotions can take us down the wrong track and we end up making things worse, for all the very best reasons.'

He fell silent and again stared out over the sea.

'It's when you're alone in your decisions that you run the greatest risk of getting it wrong.'

We finished the food and sat in comfortable silence for a while. We both leaned back in our chairs and closed our eyes.

'I never showed you the pictures,' I said. 'And I never really told you, did I? Why I felt I had to do what I did.'

When he didn't reply I opened my eyes.

He sat looking at me.

'I sort of knew anyway,' he said. 'It's a strange community, this, with its own logic. Isolated and introverted, but with strong solidarity and fierce loyalty. If you belong. People here know each other. Most have lived here all their lives, and many are related. And even if they're not, I suspect they somehow still consider themselves as family. And they look after each other, in their own way. But then there are people like you and me. We'll never belong, however much we might try, and however much we might want to. But we are respected. It's taken me a long time. You too. But we do have a place here now, and people respect us. Then there are people like Lola. She will never belong either. Or be respected. In their eyes she doesn't exist.'

'Why?'

'Well . . . she's made some fundamental mistakes. When you come here you have to obey the unwritten laws of this community. I think every society has its own. If you don't pick them up, or if you ignore them, you'll never be included.'

'And what did Lola do – or not do?'

George looked at me as if he was trying to work out how much I already knew. Or how much he should tell.

'Lola lies,' he said finally.

I wasn't able to stop an involuntary laugh.

'Lies?' I repeated.

George shook his head.

'You don't understand,' he said. 'Lola is a compulsive liar. She can't distinguish between truth and lies. And if you can't, well, then you don't know what's right and what's wrong. And then it follows that you can't follow any laws, written or unwritten.'

He looked at me again.

'I can assure you that whatever she told you, none of it is true.

Or the vital bits aren't.'

I was still incredulous. There had been moments during my conversation with Lola when I had felt that we understood each other. When I had empathised with her, even felt tenderness for this vulnerable woman. It was my turn to shake my head. I just couldn't believe it.

I began to tell George what Lola had said.

When I finished he shook his head again and smiled a crooked little smile.

'Lola did have twin girls, but they were fostered out when they were babies and later adopted. Lola hasn't seen them since they were taken from her. They're adults now. Her son died in a car accident three years ago. Her youngest daughter, Lizzie, died from an overdose shortly after Ika was born. Well, there you are . . .' George finished with a sigh.

I was speechless. I couldn't stop seeing the image of Lola's hands on the table. Hard hands, I had reflected.

'So now there is just the grandchild. And he is only there because nobody sees him either. He is on the outside, just like his grandmother. But if you ask the right people, in the right way, they know what's going on. People have seen how she behaves. Seen the boy beaten black and blue. Yet not seen him if you see what I mean. He is seen as one with his grandmother, and the loyalty and the solidarity doesn't include either of them.'

I was close to tears.

'I just thought you should know before you see CYF tomorrow. They won't be able to tell you anything, even if they know. And I'm not sure they do.'

'Thank you,' I said. 'I am not sure what to do with this information. How it changes things, if it does.'

'I think it will, but we're still looking at a long process. It's the law, and nothing can change that. It will take its time.'

'I'll have to talk to Ika,' I said. 'But I think it should wait until I know more. And I can't leave here until I'm sure Lola's not coming.'

George nodded.

'I'll keep him overnight. He's in the little sleepout behind my house. He came up to my house last night, I think, and I found him on the deck this morning after you rang. But it's not a long-term solution. Not even a temporary one. CYF will decide where to place him in the interim, while they go through their investigation. But he can stay with me until you've had your meeting. Then we'll see what they decide.'

After George had left I took a short walk on the beach, making sure I had the house in sight all the time. I waited all afternoon. When the sun sank and the wind eased I realised she probably wasn't coming. I sat on the deck wrapped in a blanket and allowed my eyes to adjust to the falling dusk.

I thought about Ika of course. And I thought about the absolute vulnerability of children. Especially small children, and children lacking the safety net that family and friends should constitute.

I thought about my brother. And I thought about myself.

It is summer and there are weeks when they are by themselves. Those weeks are good weeks. Sometimes they take walks: Mother, Marianne and Daniel. Sometimes they walk to Gärdet and Marianne and Daniel can run forever over the open fields and roll around in the grass. Such days are the very best.

She doesn't know where Hans is, and she doesn't ask.

But summer ends and school starts again. And the good days end too. Hans is back and now he sometimes spends the whole day at home. Marianne can't go to school. She can't leave Daniel. She says she has a sore stomach – and this is true. Her stomach aches and she feels sick. Sometimes she goes to school in the morning, but runs back home at lunchtime. Because that is when Mrs Andersson leaves.

If Hans is home she closes the door to the nursery and they stay in there all afternoon. Most evenings Hans goes out and then they eat in the kitchen. Mrs Andersson cooks the dinner before she leaves. After dinner Marianne and Daniel have a bath. Sometimes Mother comes and sits on the closed toilet and watches them play in the bath. And then she smiles a little.

It is Daniel's second birthday and Mrs Andersson has made a small birthday cake. It is covered with light blue marzipan and it has 'Daniel 2 years' written in red jelly on it. Two red-and-white-striped candles stand in the centre. It is the best cake Marianne has ever seen. Marianne and Mother have set the table with plates and spoons. Daniel is sitting in his high-chair at the end of the table. Marianne is just about to light the candles on the cake when she hears the front door open. They all freeze, even Daniel. Everything goes silent. Marianne holds the lit match until it burns her fingers. She blows out the flame and sinks down on her chair. They look at each other, Mother and Marianne, but nobody speaks.

Hans doesn't come into the kitchen; he goes straight to the bedroom and slams the door shut behind him. Mother watches as Marianne lifts Daniel out of his chair and sets him on the floor, but she doesn't say a word. She sits absolutely still as Marianne takes Daniel's hand and leads him back to the nursery. She lifts him up and puts him in the cot. Daniel gives a little whimper, but Marianne puts her finger to her lips and whispers 'Shhh'. Daniel smiles and does the same, and Marianne slips back to the kitchen. Mother is still in her chair and she watches while Marianne cuts three pieces of cake. She tries to get them onto the plates without them tipping over, but one falls over anyway. It means bad luck, Mrs Andersson says. Marianne uses her fingers to stand it up again, and sets the plate in front of Mother. Mother reaches out and slowly strokes Marianne's hair. Marianne stands holding the two plates for a moment, not sure what to do. In the end she does nothing, just turns around and retreats to the nursery, closing the door behind her.

She lifts Daniel out of his cot and feeds him some cake, and she eats some too. It looked better than it tastes. They play for a while. All is quiet in the apartment. It is time for Daniel to go to bed but he hasn't had his milk yet. She changes him, puts him back in his cot and tiptoes to the kitchen. Mother is no longer there and the kitchen is dark. Marianne doesn't turn on the light. She knows her way around and there is enough light from the hallway for her to heat the milk and fill the bottle. It is done quickly and she makes it back to the nursery without disturbing anything in the dark and silent apartment.

Daniel has his milk while Marianne slips out to brush her teeth and change into her nightgown. Still no sounds, but she stops for a moment just inside the nursery door and listens. Then she climbs into the cot and lies down beside Daniel. He is asleep on his back and milk is dribbling from the corner of his mouth. She bends forwards and licks it off and gives him a kiss. Then she pulls the blanket up and tucks it tightly around the two of them. She lies with her nose in Daniel's soft hair. She closes her eyes and eventually goes to sleep.

I could see them suddenly so absolutely clearly and objectively. I was still at the kitchen table and I had not turned on the light. The house was in darkness, and it felt as if it were listening, waiting. The beach beyond the window seemed to emanate its own faint light. All else was darkness.

Again, I pulled out the image from my memory. I watched the two small children clinging to each other. Because that is all they have.

I had never seen them like this before. Not even when I first read about how other people described them.

'The two terrified children, two and eight years old, were found clinging to each other in the nursery.'

When we were just married, my husband and I made a trip to Sweden. It wasn't my idea. I had never thought about returning. My early childhood slept in a sealed space in my memory and I had felt no urge to awaken it. I think perhaps my husband thought the trip would make me open up. Make me tell him more about my early life. But telling him would have forced me to tell myself. And I simply wasn't able to do that. So the trip changed nothing. We behaved like any tourists and my memories stayed safely tucked away. We stayed in a small hotel on the southern heights, a part of the city that evoked no memories at all. We did walk past the building where I had lived, but I allowed myself no reaction as I pointed it out to my husband. He said he thought it was a beautiful building and I realised he was right. Stockholm was at its most beautiful too. It was late spring, a day or two before all the greenery would burst into leaf. The trees in the parks were enveloped in a frail shimmering veil of pale green. We walked down to Strandvägen and strolled slowly along the quay. The water smelled chilly but the sun glittered on the dark surface. We crossed the bridge to Djurgården. There was the Nordic Museum, the fairytale palace from my first few months in Stockholm, the time that in hindsight seemed to have been characterised by a kind of cautious hope. I was able to think about that time, but I felt no urge to enter the museum. It was no longer a fairytale palace but a pompous building that made me feel a slight unease. It evoked thoughts of delusional grandeur and national romanticism.

A few days later we took the ferry to Åland. I could see how beautiful it was from where we stood and looked out over the sea. The bare archipelago lay in dormant anticipation, allowing the pale spring sunlight to play over the naked cliffs. The days of travel sickness that had made me dread travelling as a child were long gone, yet I felt my stomach cramp in familiar waves. I was relieved to leave Stockholm, but I was not looking forward to Åland. By then I regretted the entire trip.

We picked up a rental car in Mariehamn and drove to my grandfather's village in a little over an hour. The spring was not as advanced here as it had been in Stockholm, and despite the sunshine the air was bitterly cold. The sky was like glass.

I found Grandfather's house without difficulty. But as I stood in front of it I felt nothing. It had been repainted bright yellow and extended on two sides. It wasn't Grandfather's house. And it wasn't mine. His house lived in my memory, but it was another house, in another time. Neither existed any more. I turned around and pulled my husband with me for a walk along the deserted road. We walked down to the sea and I felt the same there. I knew that I had walked here with my grandfather, yet it felt alien. It was another place now. We stood and looked out over the shallow inlet. My husband said he found this beautiful too. And it was, of course.

On our way back to the car we passed several houses but saw not one person. Not until we reached the very last house at the edge of the village. There was a woman behind the gate. She smiled and greeted us, and we responded. When she asked if there was anything she could do for us I walked up to the gate and introduced myself. I explained why we had come. For an instant it was as if the old woman had been struck dumb, but then she clapped her hands together, cocked her head and looked at me more closely, with a gradually widening smile.

'Is it truly Marianne?' she asked.

She opened the gate and invited us in. It felt impossible to decline. She insisted on giving us a cup of coffee and we followed her inside the house. Of the two of us, it was always my husband who was the social conversant, but he knew no Swedish and was of no help here. He smiled and pulled out our chairs. I don't know what he was thinking. When the coffee had been served, the old woman sat down and the kitchen went silent. The only sound was the ticking of a clock on the wall. I had nothing to say.

I looked more closely at the woman. I didn't recognise her. But in my memories from my early childhood, there were only ever two people: my grandfather and me. There were no neighbours, no family. Just the two of us.

'Your grandfather's life was a sad one,' she said finally. 'I think we all felt that he died of a broken heart.'

She leaned forwards and took my hand.

'He was a good man, your grandfather. I want you to know that.'

Something stirred deep inside and I slowly withdrew my hand. The woman let hers rest on her lap.

'He adored her, you see. His beautiful Finnish wife. Who would have guessed there was such ugliness in that beauty? But she was a bad person. It is not right to speak ill of people, but there are some you can't find anything good to say about. She had no decency. None. There is a name for women like her, but I won't sully my mouth with it.'

The old woman looked down, as if she regretted her words.

'Good riddance, we all said when she disappeared with the baby. It was not his of course, but your grandfather would have been happy to have her and the child regardless. He was devastated. But he was left with the little girl and he had to pull himself together. For her sake. Your mother. As beautiful as her mother. Or even more so. A true beauty with her blonde hair and big blue eyes.'

She looked at me and there was kindness and compassion in her eyes. This was not idle gossip. She genuinely wanted me to know. I listened. But I realised that I heard the sounds of her speech as much as the content. In her Åland Swedish dialect the words came out soft and thoughtful, and they affected me in a way the story didn't. It was as if this language had found a crack in the emotional defence I had created. It penetrated, and it affected me painfully. I looked at my husband, even though I knew I could expect no help from him. All he could do was sit on his chair and look politely interested. But his very presence was a kind of support regardless, a reminder of who I was.

'He did die of a broken heart, that was clear for all to see. Three broken hearts, in a sense,' she continued. 'The wife first. Then the daughter. And then the grandchild. You.' She looked at me. 'He lost all three of you.'

I had nothing to say, and I didn't trust my voice anyway. So I just sipped the hot, strong coffee and tried to suppress the feelings that threatened to come gushing forth.

'Your mother was not a bad person. She was just . . . well, just too beautiful, I suppose. She wanted to be in the movies. And what she wanted, he gave her. He wasn't able to deny her anything. She was allowed to go overseas and study. Go to acting school. And when she came home pregnant he accepted that too. He didn't just accept it – no, he loved that child even before it was born, I think. And I suppose he expected her to settle down here then. That she had come home for good. I think we all thought she had. She could have had a good life here. Found a husband, even though she had the child. But you see, there must have been some of her mother's restlessness in her. And this place just wasn't for her. He should have known it wouldn't work. But he didn't. So when she went to Stockholm and left the baby here, that's when he became an old man. After that, he just lived for the little one.'

She looked at me and nodded.

'He lived just for you, that's how it was.' She nodded again as if she were talking to herself as much as to me. 'But even that little life was to be taken from him.'

I noticed that my husband was beginning to look a little restless, and I tried to make him understand that it was nearly over. But I didn't translate the woman's words.

'I have often wondered what became of you, Marianne,' she said, and patted my hand. 'Such a sweet little girl, we all thought. You adored your grandfather. As he adored you. It must have been hard for you to be taken away like that. And your grandfather died just a year or so later.'

She sighed and asked if we would like more coffee. When we declined, she slowly rose.

'I am sorry, I'm just babbling on,' she said. 'But through the years I have often thought of you and wondered how you fared. Especially when I heard about the terrible things that happened.'

She might have been hoping for a reaction from me. Perhaps she had questions she would have liked to ask, but if so, I ignored her unspoken queries. I just thanked her. For the coffee and for what she had told me. I made no comment. It felt impossible. As if something would break irretrievably if I did.

We shook hands and the old woman gave me a spontaneous firm hug. Then she took a step back, holding on to my arms.

'You might want to visit your grandfather's grave?'

When I nodded, she told me the way to the cemetery. Then she went back into the kitchen and returned with a small drawing showing where the grave was.

We thanked her again and said goodbye.

As we slowly drove past the house she was still on the front steps watching us and with her arm raised in farewell.

I never returned to Åland.

But I did go back to Stockholm when I returned from New Zealand. I was on my own then. Again it was spring, but this time it was overcast and chilly, with a few days of hard wind that brought sparse snow that felt like ice. This time I went to the Royal Library and sat down to read the newspaper articles.

'The children, two and eight years old, were found clinging to each other in the nursery.'

and

'Eight-year-old girl witness to domestic drama that takes lives of both parents.'

I didn't know what to do with that image then. There was no way I could embrace the fact that I had been so little, just a small child.

But as I sat there at the kitchen table in my now completely dark house, I finally saw it clearly. I could see her. A panic-stricken eight-year-old. The same age as Ika. How could I have placed such guilt with her? A little child.

I stood up stiffly and went to the bedroom. I lay down fully dressed and closed my eyes.

18.

I woke with a start and a feeling of having overslept. But it was only just after six. My meeting in Hamilton wasn't till eleven o'clock. I got up and had a long hot shower. Wrapped in a towel I then walked out onto the deck. The sun was shrouded in veils of pink and purple and was only just above the horizon. There was a light breeze and a sense of hope seemed to permeate the air. As if it wasn't just the beginning of a new day, but a new time.

I had just sat down to breakfast when George rang. We agreed that I was to come over when I got back from Hamilton. Meanwhile George was taking Ika fishing.

Most roads become mere routes of transportation if you use them often, but for me none of the local roads had done that. Almost always, I experienced my travel with open eyes, never ceasing to marvel at the landscape. Partly perhaps because I often took narrow secondary roads that required me to drive slowly. But mostly because I still had not become one with the place. I could still see it. This morning I had allowed myself plenty of time. I drove slowly through the softly undulating landscape, so sweetly smiling and inviting. It was difficult to believe that the rounded hills were probably volcanoes. That the pastoral grass was just a thin skin over violent forces that could in an instant erase all that man had painstakingly created.

I had over an hour to kill when I parked in Hamilton so I decided to go for a walk. I had spent almost my entire childhood and youth in an urban setting, yet even this small city felt overwhelming to me now. I realised that I no longer instinctively moved in the right direction when I met people; and several times I awkwardly dodged this way and that. The whole city seemed embedded in greenery but on foot I never reached a park or open field, and I was relieved when it was time to make my way to the meeting.

The woman I met seemed to be between forty and fifty. She had short dark hair, no makeup and she was discreetly dressed in a simple tan dress and green cardigan. She greeted me and we sat down, she behind her desk and I opposite her. A frosted glass partition separated her space from the surrounding open-plan office. It was simple and uncluttered, matching the woman well. The only slightly surprising item was a large, beautiful painting of a marine landscape on the wall behind her.

She introduced herself as Claire Peters, and she opened the conversation by saying that she was not really the person I needed to meet. She would not be directly involved, if it did indeed become a matter for CYF.

'But George Brendel is a good friend and he asked if I would meet with you informally,' she said. To my surprise she blushed, just as George had, and the blush spread over her pale face and down her throat.

'Perhaps you could begin by giving me the background,' she continued.

I pulled out my folder with my paper and the pictures and put it on the desk.

Then I began to tell her my story.

When I finished she rubbed her forehead with her fingers, as if trying to clear her thoughts.

'I assume you know that we have routines that are enshrined in law for handling matters like these. There are no exceptions. The fact that I know George and that he knows you makes no difference, of course. And since you are a party to this matter I am not able to make you privy to any information we might have about the family.'

She paused briefly.

'Perhaps it would be helpful if I described to you in general terms how we go about an investigation of this kind? Or perhaps you are already familiar with the process?'

'Well, you'd think I would know, wouldn't you? Considering I am a GP. And in a sense I do. I'm aware that I have managed this situation completely wrongly from the start. I allowed my emotions to take over. So I guess I would benefit from hearing how I should have handled it.'

She smiled briefly, then fixed her eyes steadily on me for a moment and I felt as if there was something she was trying to convey. But it might just have been my imagination.

'Believe me, I understand where you are coming from. But in emotionally charged situations it often pays to remain dispassionate, and stick to the established rules and protocols rather than act impulsively. On the other hand, there are situations where impulsive intervention is the difference between life and death.'

Once more, I felt as if her eyes were trying to convey a message that she for some reason was unable to express in any other way.

I was not sure how to interpret it.

'We are humans, with a natural instinct to try and protect the vulnerable. Our instinct tells us to act when a life is in danger. Without it, we would not be human. You are a doctor, but you are a human being first.'

She paused and looked at me again.

'I can't tell you anything about this family, but I can assure you that what you have done, though highly irregular, may have saved the boy's life. It will be taken into account when the case is investigated. And when decisions are made.'

Suddenly I felt tired. It was as if the tension that had held me together was starting to give.

'We will need to inspect the home, of course. Make our own assessment of the situation. If it is deemed necessary to remove the child immediately, we rely on approved family homes where he would be placed in the interim. If it is later decided that he needs to be placed long term, we would try to find a suitable family member who is willing to take over his care. Maintaining family bonds is a priority for us. Naturally, it's not always possible to place the child with a family member, but we always strongly encourage ongoing contact with the family. I am sure you understand that this is a process that cannot be rushed. It takes time.'

'How long?' I asked, though I knew it was a pointless question.

'It's impossible for me to give you an answer. First, from what you have told me it sounds as if the grandmother is not contactable. I don't know how long it might take us to locate her. On the surface of it, it does sound like she has abandoned the child. We often have difficulties tracing family members, especially when they are not local. When we do, we will schedule a meeting with all concerned. The hope is that it will be possible to reach a unanimous decision. But if the caregiver is unco-operative it might be difficult. Sometimes it becomes a matter for the court.'

'And during all this time he will have to stay with strangers?'

'I can assure you that the families we rely on are used to caring for severely traumatised children.'

'But this child is not just traumatised,' I said. 'In my view he is slightly handicapped. Probably mildly autistic. Whatever the reason, he has severe problems expressing himself and functioning socially. He has only just adjusted to living with me and now he is doing much better in school as well. I am sure his teacher will confirm this.'

She nodded.

'We will factor in all aspects, of course. But we make emergency placements only with previously approved families.'

My heart was throbbing and I felt that I could not trust my voice so I said nothing.

'Like I said before, we have to follow the rules. These matters are always very difficult and it is extremely important that we are sure we've made the right decision.'

She glanced at her watch.

'It's time for lunch, and I have a meeting at half past one. If you have time, perhaps we could finish this conversation over lunch? There's a nice café nearby.'

I hesitated. I felt tired. I needed to gather my thoughts. And I felt that I'd got as far as I could for now. There was nothing more to say.

'It won't be a very long lunch. And I would appreciate the company,' she said, and stood up.

I followed her through the open office, where it was obvious that it was lunchtime. Many chairs were empty.

The café was just a block or two away.

'How long have you known George?' she asked when we were seated and had placed our orders.

'Well, in a way ever since I moved here almost fifteen years ago. But in another way I don't know him at all. We're neighbours, but we have never had any close contact until very recently. I called him in desperation when I didn't know how to contact Ika's family after I rescued him from the sea that day. And since then I think George has also become an important person in Ika's life. It was George's place he fled to when he heard that his grandmother was on her way. In the end she never came, but she could show up anytime, so Ika is still staying with George. So to answer your question, I suppose it would be correct to say I don't know George at all. I know hardly anything about him. He has been kind and helpful during this time, that's all.'

She had picked up a serviette and was folding and unfolding it absent-mindedly. Then she looked up at me.

'So you don't know what happened when he first arrived here?'

I shook my head.

'Well, I don't know much either. You don't really know a person just because you know what has happened to him. I have never talked to George about what happened. But I know that he arrived here with his wife, Lidia, twenty-five years ago or more. They were young and recently married and I think they had that dream of escaping overpopulation and pollution. Beginning a new life here. But there could have been completely different reasons, of course. Anyway they bought the farm where George still lives. I think they had intended to farm the land, and they started by planting olives. They had cattle, too, then. Beef, I think.'

The waitress appeared with our food and Claire paused.

'Lidia died in a car accident. One of those road accidents that are far too common here. A heavy truck that crossed the centre line. She didn't have a chance. They said nobody saw George for a year. And he never planted anything more.'

We ate in silence for a while.

'Lidia was pregnant with their first child. She was so happy. I got to know her when we joined the same art class on Saturdays. Her English wasn't very good at first. We became friends and started to see each other now and then. Sometimes we would go out for a glass of wine or a coffee after class. She was very talented. On a totally different level to the rest of us. I'm not sure why she took the course. Perhaps it was a way for her to get out a bit. They were so isolated, and she was so lively and outgoing. For some reason I had the impression that she was the one who had money. Not that we ever talked about that. Strange, really, how much you think you know, though you couldn't exactly say how. But it's a big farm, so I guess the locals talked.'

She looked at me and she seemed to hesitate before she continued.

'Many years later we had a case here involving a child who only spoke German. It was a tragic situation and we needed someone who could interpret. Someone suggested we ring George. He was happy to help and you could see he was very good with the child. As a thank you, I took him out for lunch. I'm not sure if he remembered me – we had only met very briefly a couple of times when he had dropped off or picked up Lidia. I guess everybody knew of him, but he wouldn't have known many at all.'

'Yes, I know about that,' I said. 'I am one of those whom everybody seems to know, too,' I smiled.

'Well, on the spur of the moment I asked if he would be prepared to be a temporary caregiver,' she continued. 'He said he would give it some thought and let me know.'

She kept turning her coffee cup and gazing at it.

'When he rang to accept, I suggested another lunch. To give him more information. Well, it wasn't exactly my job . . . I suppose I just used it as an excuse. I wanted to see him. We had a few lunches. A few dinners. And a few walks. I guess I hoped it would develop over time. Turn into . . . well, something more. But time passed and it didn't. Our meetings became fewer and more infrequent until they stopped altogether. I guess nothing had ever really started.'

I saw her blush again, and I didn't know what to say.

'I just thought that perhaps you were wondering how we know each other.' She raised her glass of water and sipped it. Then she put it down and took a deep breath. And now she was her professional self again.

'I'll leave the case with one of our investigators. Naturally, I will stress the urgency. But these cases are always urgent. You should expect to hear from us by tomorrow.'

As we parted outside in the street she shook my hand and held on to it, looking straight at me.

'I'd like you to know that George is still one of our approved temporary caregivers.'

She let go of my hand.

'It was nice meeting you,' she said.

'Thank you,' I said. 'I am very grateful. For all.'

She nodded and smiled.

As I had passed through Raglan I slowed down and took the narrow road that snaked high above the sea. I found a spot where I could drive off the road and park, and went and sat on a grassy patch overlooking the sea. From here, the ocean was different from the one I lived with back home on my beach. Blindingly sparkling, turquoise blue, so intense it made the bright blue sky pale in comparison. Although I knew the waves were crashing far below, up there I could hear nothing. The sea looked alluringly peaceful, a glittering blue-green eternity. The light wind rustled the stands of flax that covered the slope below.

How would I make Ika understand when I myself didn't understand? How would I be able to comfort him when I had no comfort for myself?

Over the time we had known each other we seemed to have developed a kind of instinctive rapport. But it only worked when we were together – at home, or in the car. Just the two of us. We never talked much, but we still communicated. I rarely received more than a nod or a shake of the head from him. And even more seldom a smile. But this had come to make those words and gestures the more pregnant with meaning. There were moments, as we listened to music or worked on our project, when it seemed that there was a perfect flow of wordless communication between us.

To sit him down and try to explain what lay ahead would be difficult. If he were to be allowed to stay with George it might make things a little easier. But he would want to know how things were going to pan out long term. He deserved to know. So how was I to explain? All I had to communicate was my own anxiety. It felt as if we were equally exposed and vulnerable. Pawns in a game not of our making, and one that neither of us could influence.

Every now and then it had struck me that our relationship was at least as important to me as it was to Ika. Perhaps more so. Could it be my own situation that concerned me so, and not his?

'All will be well.'

That's what you say when you're not sure how things will turn out. To assure yourself, as much as others. Or when you know that nothing will ever in fact be well again.

To comfort yourself, as much as others.

It's the sound that wakes her. Not because it is very loud, but because it is different. Without opening her eyes she lies still, listens. Her nose is buried in Daniel's hair and she can smell his baby sweat. At first she is not sure if the sound was real. Perhaps it was a dream. Perhaps it will go away.

Then there is another heavy thud, like something hitting the wall hard. In the silence that follows she can hear some faint sounds of voices. She can't hear the words, but she can feel them. She can feel what they are saying even though she can't hear them. In a way it is worse like this.

Because although she thinks she knows what they are saying, she could be wrong. It could be something even worse . . . the worst that she is able to imagine.

Then there is an even heavier thud, and the sound of something crashing to the floor. Something falling over. And then a voice. This time it is Mother's voice, but strangely altered. She can't hear what Mother is saying, it is just a sound. There are no words; it is like the sound of an animal. Just a sound. Loud at first, then slowly it fades. It doesn't sound like Mother at all now. It is a terrible sound and she doesn't want to hear it. But even when it stops, it is as if it still hangs in the air, very faint, but still there.

Daniel sleeps through it all, and she lies very still so as not to disturb him. His warm body lies pressed against hers, but she feels cold all the same. Her mouth is dry and she needs to go to the toilet. But she stays put, her eyes closed and her arms around her baby brother.

The sound doesn't go away. She can't hear it but it is still there, she knows it is. And she will have to follow it. She climbs out of the cot and puts her cold feet on the floor. Her nightgown is damp; she is even colder now that she is no longer in bed with Daniel close. She shivers and folds her arms across her chest. She stands still, her ears alert. Then she walks out into the hall. Every now and then she stops. Listens. But there is no sound.

The door to the bedroom is ajar. She doesn't touch it. She just leans forwards and looks inside. Her teeth are chattering now. She can see a corner of the bed, a small piece of the floor. The light is on but it looks strange. It seems to wash over the floor only. The carpet is a heap half pushed under the bed. And there is Mother's arm, outstretched on the floor with her hand open. She can't see Hans but she can hear him snoring. That's all she can hear over the sound inside her head. It sounds as if her heart is inside her head. It throbs and beats louder and louder, and it feels as if her whole head will crack open.

She walks down the hall and into the kitchen. There, she pulls a chair out from under the table and carries it to the kitchen bench. She climbs up onto the chair and from there onto the cold marble benchtop, where she kneels down and stretches out her hand for one of the knives from the stand on the wall. She holds it in a tight grip as she slowly climbs down. She puts the knife on the bench and adjusts her nightgown, which has become twisted. Then she returns the chair to the table. For a moment she stands looking at the knife. She can't think. Her head is throbbing and her fingers are so cold she can't understand how they will ever bend around the handle of the knife, but when eventually she picks it up, she squeezes it firmly in her hand and returns to the bedroom.

With a light push the door opens enough for her to step inside.

The strange light is coming from one of the bedside lamps, which has fallen to the floor. It shines straight at her, blinding her at first. She blinks and the room slowly comes into view. Mother is closest. Her open hand lies next to Marianne's foot. Mother is on her back with both her arms flung wide. Her dressing gown is open and she is naked underneath it. Her head is on the side, as if she is asleep.

Hans is lying on the bed. His shirt is on the floor by the bed but he is still wearing his black trousers. And his black shoes. He is lying on his stomach, but one hand is hanging over the side of the bed and his face is turned away from her. His back is very white in the strange light that shines from below.

She sinks down to the floor and kneels beside Mother, and as she bends over, she can hear Mother breathing. But it doesn't sound right. It sounds as if there is something inside her throat – it sort of gargles. With every breath red foam seeps through her lips. It looks like blood. There is a pool of darker blood on the floor underneath Mother's head, too.

Marianne puts the knife on the floor and tries to pull Mother's dressing gown closed, but her cold hands are stiff and clumsy. She is not weeping, but her throat aches as if the weeping is stuck there.

Then Hans moves on the bed. He groans and shifts a little, but that's all. Marianne rises stiffly and turns towards the bed.

It is only the first stab that is slow.

The knife sinks into the side of Hans's neck and it seems to take a long time. There is so much blood. It is going everywhere. All over the bed. Hans flings out his arms, and again and again he tries to rise, but each time he slumps back down. She plunges the knife, again and again – anywhere. Finally Hans slides halfway down onto the floor. Quickly, she has to take a step backwards. Her foot slides on the floor and she slips and falls. She lands close to Mother; she can feel Mother's body beside her.

She can hear someone sob but she doesn't know who.

She lies beside Mother on the floor. Her chest hurts. It is as if something is stuck inside it too. It hurts to breathe, and she takes quick little gasps of air. All the while she keeps her eyes closed.

She feels Mother stir. She opens her eyes and looks at her, watches her slowly reach out for Marianne's hand, which rests on the floor between them. Mother gently prises the knife from Marianne. Then she drops her hand back down to the floor again. Now Mother is clasping the knife.

When she looks at Mother's face it is almost as if she is trying to nod. But then there is nothing, nothing at all. All is very still, and Marianne watches the red foam trickle through Mother's lips and down her cheek.

Marianne rises, first onto all fours, then she stands up. She walks slowly towards the door, and when she looks back she can see the red prints from her feet.

She is shaking, and there is nothing she can do to make it stop. She is wet and she knows she has peed herself. Still, she walks straight to the nursery and climbs into the cot. Daniel is asleep, but he whimpers a little as she adjusts herself behind him and puts her arms around him.

She slides her hand underneath his pyjama top and lets her fingers run over the scar under his arm, while at the same time burying her nose in his neck.

Eventually she falls asleep.

19.

Reluctantly, I got up and went back to the car. I drove slowly, even slower than usually. I rolled down the window and let the breeze in. The sea was a background to everything, a constant presence far below to my right.

I had driven to Hamilton filled with a complex mix of feelings. Returning, I felt different. The future was still unknown, but I realised I could finally see myself, and my actions, more clearly.

I had allowed Ika's life and his needs to become intrinsically interwoven with my own. In the end, perhaps I had become unable to distinguish between the two. I had seen him and, in a sense, seen myself. Taken for granted that I understood him and that I knew what was best for him. What was it George had said? Things often turn out badly if we allow ourselves to be guided by our feelings.

Perhaps particularly so if they are our deepest subconscious feelings. I had found Ika, and in him I thought I had found myself. And despite wanting to care for him, perhaps I had ignored his real needs. Strong feelings often breed a kind of benign arrogance: my passionate heart must not be questioned. I feel, therefore I *know*. All my education, my entire adult life experience was just a thin scab over my bleeding child's heart.

I tried to argue with myself. Convince myself that the matter was now in good hands. Still, my resistance was formidable. It refused to withdraw completely.

'Trust me, trust us, all will be well.'

A gnawing doubt still lingered.

As I drove up to my house I saw George's car parked at the back, and when I walked around the corner I found him on the deck. He was pacing back and forth. When he spotted me he came running down the steps.

'He has disappeared!' he said. 'He wanted to come here and wait for you, but when I came down to check on him he wasn't here. I thought I saw tyre tracks in the sand behind the house, and I thought Lola might have come after all.'

I stared at him. The slight sense of relief and hope that had filled me instantly dissolved.

'We went fishing, but we didn't even get a nibble and we both got bored. On our way back he said he wanted to stay here and wait for you. I should have stayed too, but he didn't seem to want me around. I didn't think there was any harm in leaving him here.'

George was staring out over the sea. Then he looked down.

'I rang CYF straight away but there's not much they can do right now. I rang you too, but I just got your voicemail.'

I pulled out my mobile from my pocket. It was turned off.

'I've been running back and forth along the beach since then.

Shouting his name and searching. But I can't find him. I haven't even seen any footprints anywhere.'

His voice broke and he seemed close to tears.

Had Ika really run down to the beach? The beach was endless. Prints could be erased in an instant. And the sea swallowed all in its way.

A little frightened child could disappear without a trace.

I opened the door and went inside. The place looked as I had left it. There were no signs of violence. I went into the lounge and I noticed the piano lid was open. I wasn't sure whether it had been when I left, but I didn't think so. The curtain to Ika's room was closed. I pushed it aside and looked. The bed looked untouched – no signs of him there.

I wasn't weeping, but I heard myself whimpering quietly under my breath as I tried to think. It was likely George was right. That Lola had indeed showed up at last, and had taken him. But part of me wouldn't believe it. Ika was very sensitive to sounds. He would have realised it was not my car. He would have run.

Or was I once again projecting myself onto Ika? Could I really be so sure I knew what he would have done? Perhaps he had just stayed here at the piano, paralysed with fear? On the other hand, we could be completely wrong, both George and I. Perhaps Ika had just set off on one of his little walkabouts.

George stood in the doorway.

'I'm so sorry,' he said. 'It's all my fault. I should have kept him with me all the time.'

'That's just not possible,' I said. 'You can't keep him when he is set on going. He demands space and freedom. He knew you were there, at home, waiting for him. That's all he needed. It's not your fault.'

'I'll take another look along the beach,' he said and turned around.

'I'll go the other way,' I said.

The sun was low and the landscape rested in a kind of stillness despite the constant crashing of the waves onto the empty beach. I jogged over the cool, wet sand. All the while I kept calling his name.

Eventually I had to slow down. The sun sank below the horizon in a blood-red crescendo that left a slowly fading aftermath of purple and grey. I suddenly realised where I was heading. I was walking up the beach, away from the sea. It was dusk now, but my eyes had adjusted and I had no problem finding my way.

I stood on the peak of a sand dune and looked down over our project. I was still struggling to get an idea of the totality of it, but from this perspective I thought I could discern something of what Ika had imagined. I walked down. When I reached the centre I lay down on the sand. Here, it was still warm from the sun. I stretched out my arms and looked up at the sky. Slowly, slowly I could detect stars in the darkening sky. Finally, I could see the entire Milky Way as a broad shimmering white ribbon across the sky. I had never seen it like this before.

I must have dozed off because his presence woke me. Ika was lying beside me on the sand. Not close, of course, but closer than I had come to expect. Without turning my head I stretched out my hand so that it rested open on the sand between us. To my utter surprise, I briefly felt his cold, scrawny hand touch mine. Then I turned to him and pulled him towards me, and held him. And he allowed it.

For a moment, I held him in my arms.

Then we lay there, side by side, and I told him where I had been. What I thought was going to happen.

I didn't say everything would be fine.

But I told him that I loved him. That I would never leave him. Whatever happened to us, he could know that I would be there. That I would never let anybody hurt him. I promised what I could promise, but no more.

Then we were silent and looked at the sky for quite a while.

'I just wanted to be here,' he said. 'I didn't think we would be able to finish it now.'

'Of course we will,' I said.

We both sat up and I looked at him.

'I think we should go back now and tell George, because he has been looking for you all afternoon.'

Ika made no reply of course.

'Do you think we should ask George for dinner?'

No reply.

'What shall we cook?'

'Soup,' he said. And we both chuckled.

It was the first time I heard Ika laugh.

20.

It was a very successful evening. I made soup out of what I had: a few potatoes, tomatoes, onions and spinach. And I made an improvised unleavened bread to go with it.

George had returned home briefly, and came back with his hair wet and a couple of bottles of wine.

We set the table on the deck, although it was completely dark, and Ika helped, lighting lots of little candles. I brought out some blankets, and went back to the kitchen and opened my laptop. I clicked on the folder where I had collected the music Ika and I had discovered together.

'Peace Piece'.

The music flowed softly through the open window and out onto the deck.

I turned off the light in the kitchen and through the window the deck appeared almost magical, lit only by the flickering candles. Ika was sitting beside George. I couldn't see what it was that had caught their interest, but they sat bent over the table, their heads close together. In the faint yellow light the scene looked like a painting. I stood still, watching, enveloped in the soft music.

I returned to the deck and sat down opposite them. Every now and then I sneaked a look at Ika. It seemed as if he had grown. As if he had made a leap in his development since the last time I saw him. He smiled quick little smiles but he never quite looked at me. He ate with his usual good appetite.

'Very tasty soup,' George said as he put down his spoon. Ika nodded and it felt like a great compliment. I cleared the table. All I had to offer for dessert was a few peaches and a small piece of cheese, which I placed on a plate and took outside.

Eventually Ika wandered over to the hammock and climbed into it. George covered him with a blanket.

We sat at the table all evening. When the music stopped we could hear the invisible sea in the darkness beyond the house.

Then George said: 'I don't know if Claire mentioned that I am an approved temporary caregiver. An unusual one, I suppose, since I am not a family, I'm just me. But over the years I have accepted quite a few emergency placements. Often of non-English-speaking children. My first language is German, but I speak a few others too. That's how it started. They needed someone who spoke German.'

I nodded.

'If you think it's a good idea, I can offer to care for Ika during the investigation. It will not be a sacrifice at all – I have become attached to him too. And it seems like he has accepted me. It's not a given that they will place him with me; there might be another caregiver that they think more suitable. But I can certainly offer. If you like.'

'That sounds absolutely perfect,' I said. 'I can't think of a better solution.'

'Agreed, then,' he said. He got up and slowly walked over to the deck railing, and stood looking out into the darkness.

'You have a wonderful home,' he said with his back to me.

An involuntary quick laugh escaped me.

'This?' I was incredulous.

'Yes,' he said. 'It feels alive. It's a little messy . . .'

He turned and looked at me.

'Sorry.'

I laughed again. 'But it is!' I said.

'Sure, it's messy. And it's not in the best condition. But it's alive. My home is a mausoleum.'

I was stunned.

'My home died with my wife,' he said quietly. 'Since then, there has been no life whatsoever there. I have cleaned it and cared for it, the way you look after a grave. With love and grief. But life hasn't come into it. Rather the opposite. It's Lidia's home, not mine.'

'Strange,' I said after a little while. 'That's how I think about my home. That all it is, is a monument to what I have lost. To me, there is no life here at all. At least there wasn't till Ika entered my life. My home was just a refuge. I was thinking about that earlier. How I have neglected my home. Or rather, how I have never even created one. Yours, I find very much alive.'

George turned back and leaned over the railing.

'Everything looks different from the outside. You can be completely mistaken. Or perhaps we can only see things through our own eyes. Perhaps nothing is absolute, and everything fills different needs for different people. The same house can be a refuge or a prison, depending on who is seeing it.'

He wandered over to the hammock and stood for a while looking down at the sleeping Ika.

'I think it's time for us to say thank you and make our way home,' he said.

We both helped, lifting Ika and wrapping him in the blanket. Then George held him in his arms. I looked at them and for a fraction of a second I felt a stab of envy. As if I wanted it to be me that George was carrying in his arms. Carrying away from here to somewhere else, somewhere warm and safe.

We stood facing each other, and George looked at me with a thoughtful expression. But in the flickering half-light it was difficult to guess what he was thinking. And I certainly hoped it was impossible for him to tell what I was thinking.

I turned and led the way around the house, shining a torch to guide us. I opened the back door of George's car and he carefully placed Ika on the seat.

'Thank you, Marion, it's been a great end to an interesting day,' he said.

'Thank *you*,' I said. 'Thank you for everything.'

There was a pause and the silence seemed to spread and keep us where we were, facing each other and with the light from the torch a bright reflecting pool on the sand at our feet.

George stroked my arm, then turned abruptly and jumped into the car.

'See you tomorrow,' he said through the rolled-down window.

I stood and watched as he drove away. I watched until the rear lights became two red pinpricks in the compact darkness.

Then I turned off the torch and waited until my eyes had adjusted to the dark.

I walked past my house and on down to the beach, and sat on the cool sand.

Here, I realised that the darkness was not absolute. From up there on the deck the sea had been one with the surrounding darkness. But now I saw a multitude of shifting grey hues, as manifold as the most colourful landscape.

They do not stay in the motel in Kawhia. By the time they arrive it is after midnight. The town seems asleep and the eating places are closed.

Instead, they drive to a camping ground on the waterfront and manage to negotiate a space for the four-wheel drive overnight, and three days for Marion's car.

Michael opens the back door of the four-wheel drive, jumps up and sits, his legs hanging off the edge. He pulls her up beside him. They sit side by side and dine on baked beans out of tins with melting peanut slabs for dessert. It is a still, warm evening.

'Are you okay sleeping here tonight?' he asks, indicating the space where they are sitting. 'Sorry, but I think it's the easiest. I often do when it's late and it seems like too much of an effort to put up the tent. If you like, I am happy to sleep on the front seats and you can have this to yourself.'

He smiles and begins to clear the space behind them. Then he jumps down and walks around the side of the car and pulls forwards the backrest of the back seat, almost doubling the sleeping space. He unrolls a mattress across the floor, but it covers barely half.

'Sorry, it's not the most comfortable, I guess,' he says. 'Feel free to rummage through my things and see if you find anything useful to pad it a bit.'

When they are finished they have created a good-sized sleeping space that looks quite inviting. They sit on top of the bedding sipping lukewarm vodka, smoking.

'I don't know what to ask about you,' he says.

'Well, you asked me to come on this trip. That's all you need to ask, I think. For the rest you can observe and develop your own impression . . .'

'Isn't that what people do when they have just met? Ask each other the most basic questions? I mean, for all I know you could be a serial murderer. I know nothing about you and have just invited you to share my bed.'

She laughs, again surprised at the ease with which it emerges.

'Ah, well. What does it matter? If I am a serial murderer I'm not likely to tell, am I? And if you ask me how old I am I will definitely lie,' she says.

'How old are you?' he asks.

There is a slight pause before she answers.

'Thirty-six,' she replies.

'There you go, that's not a lie, is it?'

She shakes her head.

'No.'

'And are you a serial murderer?'

'No,' she says, laughing again. It's extraordinary how it seizes her, this strange light joy.

He leans back, resting on his elbows.

'Tell me what you love,' he says.

She has no answer to this question. He looks at her intently, as if her response were important. He is serious now, no longer joking and smiling. Something is biting her legs and she pulls them up and folds them under her.

'Sandflies,' he says when she scratches her ankles. He sits up and reaches inside his backpack. 'Here, take this.'

He throws her a bottle of insect repellent.

'I haven't forgotten the question,' she says as she applies the repellent to her feet and legs. 'I just don't know how to answer. You tell me – what do you love?'

He lies back on the pillows that they have created out of clothes, hands clasped behind his head.

'Love is supposed to be very different from like, isn't it? A different magnitude altogether. The way I see it, love is a mental state. An elevated state where things become . . . well, more intense. Different from all other states. It's like you get a completely different perspective on everything. It hits you and lifts you up, and there is nothing you can do about it. It invades you like a bug, I suppose. And when you are afflicted it colours everything. And in some cases it can never be cured.'

He sits up, resting on his elbows again.

'Your turn!'

'I don't know . . . For me it has been more about protecting myself from love. Treading cautiously, I guess, and staying in control. Making sure I didn't catch it, perhaps.'

She frowns as if she has heard her own words and is bothered by them.

He turns on his side, resting his head in his cupped hand, looking at her.

'Well then, tell me about what you like instead.'

She thinks he is trying to make her comfortable, free her from having to expound on what she has said.

'No, I'd like to explain how I feel about love,' she says. 'I think I agree with you, really.'

She turns her gaze towards the solid darkness outside.

'It's just that I don't know much about it. To continue your metaphor, it's as if I was vaccinated against it a long time ago. I am quite simply immune.'

'I don't think that's possible,' he says. 'There's no vaccine against this bug. You've just not been exposed to the infection. If that is what it is.'

She laughs, but this time it takes an effort.

'Now, tell me three things that you like,' he says, changing the subject. 'I need to know a little about you before we take off tomorrow.'

She thinks for a moment.

'I like blood oranges. And the smell of mimosa. The sound of blackbirds singing in the spring. Not very useful information, I suppose.'

Now she smiles easily. 'You?'

'Well, I like my mother's pancakes.' He smiles and looks at her. 'And my job. But that's bordering on love. And I like lying here looking at you.'

She smiles.

'But I think that's getting borderline too.'

'We'd better call it quits then,' she says. 'It's really late.'

When he asks if she would like him to sleep in the front, she asks if he would be more comfortable in the back.

He looks at her for a moment, considering her question.

'You know, I could say that I would, just because I want to stay here and look at you.'

She tells him that will be just fine, and she listens to her own words and marvels.

She lies awake well after he has gone to sleep. Now it is she watching him, not the other way around.

And she loves it.

In the morning he is gone when she wakes. Stiffly she climbs out of the car and walks over to the communal showers. When she returns he has cleared the back of the car and laid out takeaway coffee and scones on a towel. The sun has just risen, but it hasn't yet appeared over the hills and the cool of the night still lingers in the air.

They sit down cross-legged and have their breakfast.

'It would be easier to catch the boat across, but I think we should drive,' he says. 'I have asked permission to drive out onto the peninsula, just to be sure. It's Maori land and I always make a point of respecting local interests and traditions wherever I go. I am aware of the fact that I am a guest here.'

The coffee is hot and strong, the scones fresh. It is a superb breakfast.

'We'll need to stock up a little before we leave Kawhia,' he says. 'I have plenty of food of the standard of last night's dinner, but I thought we should add some fresh stuff. Particularly since it's my birthday tomorrow. I expect a great celebration.'

He laughs.

'Let's get going!'

They finish breakfast and pack up and take off.

Kawhia lies sleepy in the early morning light. The sea is calm and a little further out the sun reaches the surface, sending playful flashes of light in all directions. Michael has made arrangements with a local farmer, and when they stop in Kawhia he is already waiting. He comes over, carrying a box with milk and eggs, fruit and vegetables.

'How do you know all these people? How do you know who to contact?' she asks as they head out of town.

He grins, his eyes on the road.

'I don't know, really, but it's a very hospitable place, this country. I always talk to the locals everywhere I go. I guess it's small enough for people to know each other, have connections around the country. So each place I go, I arrive with referrals from the previous place. It's like a chain reaction. And I have only ever met generosity and kindness. Extraordinarily so, sometimes. I've had problems with my car, and I've always found someone to help me, usually refusing to take any money. I had a break-in once. It was stressful because they took my camera. But the people of the town where it happened sort of gathered together and found all my stuff and brought it back. I have no idea how, but I guess that's the sign of a small place. People know each other. I've had a lot of help. In my experience, most people are kind and helpful if you are respectful. More so than in other parts of the world, I reckon.'

He has warned her it will be a rough journey, particularly beyond the Taharoa settlement. From there on, there are no proper roads.

I don't know what's involved. I'm so ignorant I can't even worry. I just have to trust him, she thinks and looks at his hands on the steering wheel. He seems very comfortable, whistling softly.

It's early afternoon by the time they reach Taharoa. For most of the way they have had the road to themselves. Here, too, it's very quiet. They drive

162

past vast areas of black sand. The whole landscape looks like a gigantic moon crater.

'Don't look,' he says as he skilfully navigates the car off the road to make way for an enormous transport truck, loaded with a bulldozer. She realises the truck would not have been able to stop, or give way. Black dust lingers in the air as it passes.

'It's an open mine where they extract iron from ironsand. Controversial, like most mining in this country.'

From Taharoa there is no road really. They drive along little more than a dirt track. She is sitting upright, trying to follow the snaking track with her eyes and anticipate each bump and turn, conscious of a tightness in her stomach. She is not anxious about his driving, she is just worried she will not be able to control her mounting nausea.

But soon they have left the settlement and the mining behind, and are out onto open land. The track straightens. It is windswept and wild and it looks deserted. He lowers the windows and the wind flows through. She feels better and relaxes in her seat.

They stop for lunch on a hill and they can see the sea in the distance.

Afterwards, she lies back on the grass. She has lost track of where she is, how she arrived here, even who she is. She no longer has any connection with anything else. Her previous life seems vague and distant. She is just here, and it feels as if it could last forever.

In the late afternoon they arrive at the coast. When they get out of the car they see a cluster of simple wooden houses with rusted iron roofs. They are small and seem vulnerable where they sit, set off against the endless sea behind. At the same time they exude an air of courage and resilience, as if they have managed to withstand the elements for a very long time. She can see no signs of civilisation, apart from the houses themselves – no poles indicating electricity supply or phone connection. She wonders if people actually live there. Then she spots someone walking between two of the houses, a silhouette against the sky.

The wind has picked up and sweeps across the grassy slopes ahead of them.

'Almost there,' he says. 'Just one more short leg, and then we'll stop and put up the tent.'

'How can you be so sure where we're going?' she asks. 'You've never been here before, have you?'

He grins.

'Intuition. Male intuition,' he says. 'Trust me.'

And she does, absolutely.

21.

It had turned rather cold, but strangely I still felt warm as I wandered back to the house from the beach. A few candles were still flickering and I left them to burn out. It had been a long day, and I was tired. But not sleepy. I lingered for a moment leaning on the kitchen bench and looking out. The sea had reverted to being just a sound in complete darkness, and as the candles went out, one after the other, there were no lights at all.

After a while I walked into the bedroom. Instead of lying down I opened one of the wardrobes. I pulled up a chair and climbed onto it. Even from the chair, I could only just reach the box.

It was smaller than Ika's box and I realised that he had more mementoes than I did. My box was the size of a large envelope. Inside was just one object.

A copy of *Time* magazine.

There is time for a walk before darkness falls. They stroll slowly; this is not a hike with a specific goal in mind. The landscape is barren, with softly rounded treeless hills. From a distance the grassy hills look like emerald velvet scrunched by a giant hand. Up close, the vegetation is much rougher though, the grass interspersed with thorny gorse and sharp flax. It feels as if she can see forever, and land and sea are equally endless.

Suddenly he points to the sky. They stop in their tracks and look up. High above, pencilled against the afternoon sky, a fragile veil undulates, constantly shifting its shape.

'There they are, our godwits. Kuaka.'

The tiny black specks are birds. But from this distance they make up a wondrous drifting whole of strange beauty.

'I wonder why they are called godwits,' he says. 'Is it God and then wits like the Old English word for know? God knows? Is that what it means? If so, why?'

'God knows,' she says and her new, easy laughter lifts towards the sky.

They sit on the grass and watch as the veil of birds gracefully sweeps and sways over them.

Then she feels his hand on her neck, lifting her hair. It runs over her shoulder and clasps it, pulling her close.

Has she expected this? Willed it, even?

She doesn't know.

Her body seems to know what her mind doesn't.

When he kisses her, it is the most natural thing in the world. In this magical world that she has entered this can happen. Perhaps this is the very purpose. There is no point trying to resist.

Nor does she.

She lifts her hands and holds his face, looking into his eyes. They are grey, and she thinks she can see herself reflected in them. Then she kisses him again.

He takes one of her hands and holds it. Opens it and kisses her palm.

'God knows,' he says, smiling. 'Magical things are put in our way. All we have to do is watch out for them. Take what is offered.' He kisses her hand again.

She laughs, lifts her face to the sky, exposing her throat. He kisses it.

Later, they walk back and begin to cook dinner. He gets his little barbecue going.

'No open fires here – too dangerous,' he says.

Unpacking the farmer's box they had found meat, too. Two small lamb racks and a large chunk of bacon.

While the lamb racks cook he makes a salad and she opens them a beer each.

'These are the last cold ones, so savour it,' he says. 'From here on it's lukewarm beer or red wine.'

She sits on the grass sipping the beer, watching his hands chopping and mixing the salad, turning the meat. She remembers the initial moment, when she first found him. How she had seen him as an object. As perfect as a smooth pebble or a polished piece of driftwood. Something she instinctively felt an urge to run her hand over.

So this is what she does. She bends forwards and runs her hand over his back. His hands are busy tossing the salad and there is nothing he can do but let her have her way. The skin on his back is warm, and along the spine there are tiny beads of sweat. She kisses him between the shoulderblades.

Then he drops what he is doing, turns and kisses her.

I sat on the bed with the magazine on my lap. I had turned off the ceiling light and I had not bothered turning on the one on the bedside table. I didn't really need any light. This, I could read with my hands. I had not opened the magazine, and I sat with my palm resting on the cover. I knew what the picture looked like. I could sense every detail through my hand.

It was a picture of me. Yet it wasn't me, not me at all. It was a picture of a woman who trusted her feelings and her instincts. Someone who believed that miraculously, life could take a sharp turn and open a new world. A world where godwits drifted above and laughter lifted effortlessly from her lips.

An absolutely unsustainable world.

She gets used to the camera. It becomes an extension of him and she is relaxed. She feels that she is beginning to see what he sees. His lens and her eyes seem to focus on the same spots. Except when the lens is pointed at her of course. But she gets used to that too. She begins to think she can see herself through his eyes. The camera becomes a vital part of their communication. He lets her use it too, but more and more it is enough for her just to let her eyes follow the camera. She can see what it sees. Not once is she tempted to take out her own camera.

After dinner they sit outside the tent as a full moon slowly rises beyond hills that are a black horizon. It emerges in the east, initially very large and a deep orange yellow. He pulls her close and she sits between his legs, resting her head against his chest. He puts his arms around her. Asks her if she is cold. How could she be? She thinks she will never be cold again.

Later, when the moon is high in the sky, shining with a clear white light, they climb into the tent.

Next morning he is gone when she wakes up, but she can hear him moving around outside the tent. Lighting the barbecue. She listens; there is no part of her body that is not involved. She has never been this alert. This alive. Eventually, when she smells coffee, she disentangles herself from the sleeping bag and joins him outside. He is sitting by the barbecue, hands around his knees and eyes on the sea. It must have rained overnight, though she had not noticed. The grass is wet and there are small pools of water trapped in the pockets of tent canvas along the ground. It is clear now, though, not a cloud in the newly washed sky where the veil of godwits again floats gracefully. As she sits down beside him, he points to it.

'I wonder if they are practising. Preparing for the long journey,' he says.

They drink coffee, then set off for a walk down to the sea. The hike is longer than she has anticipated but she doesn't mind. She walks behind him, watching his body as he moves at an easy, comfortable pace. She falls into the same rhythm, effortlessly following in his footsteps.

They stop when they reach the sea. They stand looking down on it, and the swell is majestic, overwhelming.

'We'll find a good spot to get into the water,' he says, scanning the shore below. 'Over there.' He points to a cluster of black rocks covered in sharp mussel shells. The rocks shelter a small lagoon of clear water. The waves break violently against the outside of the rocks, and fill the air with a spray of salt water, but the pool is calm and protected.

'You go,' he says, nodding to the water. 'I'll guard you from up here.'

And she does. This new woman undresses, climbs down and slides into the water. It is cool but she lets herself sink down, emerging out of breath. She holds on to a rock and shakes the water out of her hair. The air is filled with drops of water glistening in the sun.

When she looks up he has the camera pointed at her. She lets go of the rock and floats. Smiling.

In my dark bedroom I was there again. I licked my lips, and I was surprised when they didn't taste of salt. Suddenly I knew that it was possible to remember this isolated moment and cherish it. This one, shimmering moment belonged to me.

I had accepted that all the dark memories were mine. But I had never realised that the beautiful ones were mine too. I had a right to them. And the right to embrace them, regardless of what happened before and after. I had a right to my happiness, as well as my grief.

I stretched out my hand and turned on the bedside lamp.

22.

I slept restlessly and woke early. During that darkest hour of the late night, the hour the Chinese call the liver hour, when death seems close and life precarious, I had lain awake.

I had thought about Ika. I tried to look at myself objectively. Had I used him? Was he simply a tool for me to give my soul peace? Redeem myself? Could I ever isolate my feelings for Ika from my past? See him as he was, see *his* true needs, not my own?

I cared for him. I loved him. But the 'I' was the person shaped by the life that had been mine.

Perhaps I should abandon my attempt at being allowed to care for him?

But the grim, grey hour passed, and I fell asleep again.

When I woke, it was raining. Strangely, it felt comforting.

Energising. I got out of bed and went into the kitchen.

To my surprise Ika was sitting at the table. I had not heard him arrive, but he was a master at moving soundlessly.

He had set the table for two, with mugs and plates, butter and jam. As I sat down he leapt over to the bench and popped two slices of bread into the toaster.

Then he sat down again.

If I had thought it possible, I would have thought that he looked expectant.

'What a great beginning to the day,' I said. 'But where is George? Does he know you're here?'

Ika nodded.

I looked at the clock. It was half past six.

The toast jumped out of the toaster and Ika dashed over to collect it. Then he picked up the kettle. I watched anxiously as he held it with both his hands and balanced it back to the table and put it down.

'Can I start?'

He nodded.

He watched while I buttered a piece of toast. He had the look of a concerned cook, waiting to hear the verdict of a guest.

'Wonderful,' I said. 'To have someone cook you breakfast is the best.'

Then he finally served himself and we ate in silence for a moment.

'What do you think about this house?' I asked after a little while.

'Good,' he said.

'It needs cleaning, don't you think?'

He shrugged his shoulders.

'The only tidy place is your room.'

No comment.

'I'm going to have a go at it today. Try and get some order in our house.'

Our house.

Some days start out well, and only get better. Just as we had finished clearing the table, George arrived. When I told him I planned to start cleaning up my house he offered to help. I watched them, Ika and George, where they stood close to each other, looking back at me with an expression of anticipation. So I accepted the offer and put them to work.

It rained until midday, then the sun broke through the clouds. We took a break and sat down to have lunch on the deck. The sun glistened on the water where it had collected in drops and pools. Everything felt hopeful.

There was even less in my barren pantry now, but I managed to cook an omelette with tomatoes and potatoes. We were hungry, all three, I think, and we savoured the simple food.

We lugged out heaps of rubbish. Even though I had cleared some things in order to make a room for Ika, I had not made an effort to discard much. I had just shifted my rubbish around. But now it went. The heap behind the house grew, and George promised to get his van later and take it all to the dump.

Then we began the cleaning. George vacuumed, I mopped and Ika dusted. We worked swiftly, and it felt surprisingly satisfying. Shortly after four, we seemed to be finished.

Everything looked different. My home had gained a different persona. Or perhaps it was my perspective that had changed. It felt like removing a garment that you have worn for ages just to keep warm, and discovering that it is beautiful. I walked through the rooms and it felt as if I were seeing them for the first time. In my bedroom I spotted the magazine, still sitting on my bedside table. I walked over and put it in a drawer. I wondered if Ika or George had seen it.

'I liked it as it was,' George said. 'But even things that are naturally beautiful are even more so when clean and tidy. What do you say, Ika?' He put his hand on Ika's head, as if it were the most natural thing to do. To my surprise, Ika made no attempt to withdraw. He allowed George's hand to pat him and tousle his hair.

I looked at George but I saw no sign of his having realised how extraordinary this was.

'I think we should go for a swim,' he said.

Good idea, we all thought, and I went to collect some towels.

George went to his car and returned with two body-boards. They looked brand new.

It had been a long time since I had swum in the ocean. Although the sea was present in practically all my activities, at least as a background, I almost never swam in it. Here, it wasn't recommended to swim alone. Rips and unpredictable waves made it too risky – you were supposed to have company.

I had never felt lonely before, but as I stood there on the beach watching George and Ika throw themselves into the waves on their boards, I realised for the first time how lonely I had been. So lonely I had stopped swimming. My aloneness had never bothered me; I hadn't even been aware of it. But now it overwhelmed me. The awareness washed over me with painful sharpness and deep grief. Now that I had company.

And that was how it had been with the love of my life. Not until I experienced love did I realise what I had been living without. I had lived without love for so very long, never aware of its absence. Never once missing it. Unless the restlessness that pushed me to divorce my husband could be regarded as an unconscious stirring. A blind step away from something unsatisfactory, but with no clear direction.

When it was all over, I could have answered Michael's impossible question.

It is at the point of transition that awareness is created. The step into another state changes everything. As long as I was living in a state of ignorance, I had functioned. But I had not lived.

As I stood clutching the towels I knew I could not give up this. I could never accept being alone again.

Then I let go of the towels and ran towards the sea.

We had dinner at George's house that evening.

'I'm not a great cook, not like you, but I have a full pantry,' he said when we parted. He took Ika with him and they drove off.

I went inside for a shower. Wrapped in my towel, I poured myself a glass of wine and sat down on the deck.

I stroked my arms. I realised it was no longer a young woman's skin. Strange, I thought, how you live inside your body and take for granted that it will forever be the same. And it is, yet it is not. All that I was, was carried inside my body, yet it had little resemblance to the body of the girl or the woman who featured in my memories. The little girl walking with her hand in her grandfather's. That was me. The distraught girl on the ferry to Stockholm. The girl shivering in her wet and bloodied nightgown – that was me too.

The woman with the easy laughter, she was also me.

I turned the wine glass in my hands and stared out over the sea. And I saw all the different pictures. All the different versions of me. And I felt such tenderness. They all belonged to me, and I had a space for each and every one. They were all me. I was all of them. The sum of them.

I went and got the magazine and put it in front of me.

She looked at me with the same intensity.

I let my finger follow the features of her face.

It looked as if she had just turned her head, as if someone had called her name. Called it lovingly. Her wet hair had been caught just as it was being flicked back, sweeping around her head and filling the air with glittering droplets. She was looking over her shoulder, a look filled with laughter. Such an easy, natural laughter, and it seemed to embrace every part of her, fill all the space around her.

She was me.

When they return, it's time for lunch. He fries bacon and scrambles eggs, and from where she sits watching, the smell is heavenly. They sit in their low deckchairs and eat slowly. It is as if they are trying to draw out every moment. The beer is lukewarm by now, but it is still another perfect meal.

She knows he has a meeting scheduled with an elderly local man who has agreed to be interviewed. And photographed. She is curious to see how he works, but she has a feeling that this is something he wants to do on his own, so she suggests that he go without her. She has things to do. Whatever they may be. How can she bear to be away from him for even a few minutes?

She knows she was right, for he nods. And smiles. And says he won't be long. He takes the car and drives off.

The sense of loneliness is terrible. How can this be? She is a thirty-six-year-old woman, used to living without company. Used to managing herself and her time efficiently. But here she sits and can't think what to do. She just waits. She is helplessly exposed to something she can't control, can't understand. Something that makes her behave utterly senselessly.

It is his birthday, and she has nothing to give him. She sits on the ground by the entrance to the tent, her arms around her knees, thinking. Then she crawls inside and pulls out her backpack, opens it and digs around until she finds what she is looking for. The CD she bought in Singapore. Bill Evans. She had recognised the cover when she spotted it in a store, and had thought of Brian. It was an old recording, one of Brian's favourites that had become hers too. Or perhaps it was the whole thing, the entire situation, not just the music, that she had come to love so much. To sit in Brian's lap, listening to the soft music, not talking at all, evening after evening during that early time. Their special song had become 'Peace Piece', the third to last. They had played it so often the record was worn and often skipped. It was as if this music had become the fragile cord that kept her attached to life. And slowly, slowly, to this music, she had begun to live again.

It is the right gift today.

She takes his little pocket-knife and goes for a walk to cut some flax. In Auckland she had seen little baskets woven out of the tall sharp Phormium *leaves. They grow in abundance and she finds what she needs quickly. The sky is high and clear and completely empty. No godwits today. Perhaps they have left. But she finds a couple of small feathers and picks them up. She doesn't know if they are godwit feathers but she likes to think they are. Just like on the first day, her walk turns out to be much longer than she intended. It is as if this landscape sucks her in completely. Makes her forget time and space.*

Herself.

When finally she gets back she sits down on the ground and begins the work. It is harder than she thought. The leaves are sharp and stiff. She splices them into narrow strips and rubs them to try and make them a little softer and easier to work. Then she lays the strips on the ground and begins to plait them. She has imagined a small flat folder for the CD and the result is not far off. She sticks the CD into the folder and closes it with one of the feathers. She has just finished when she hears the car, and pops the gift into her backpack.

Before dinner they walk down to the beach again.

This time he goes into the water first and she sits on the slope above with the camera. She can get close, closer than ever. But she takes no pictures, she just watches. And again she feels this urge to run her hands over his skin. She puts down the camera, undresses and joins him.

When they get back he lights the barbecue. Then he walks over to the

177

car and returns with a package wrapped in plastic. A grin on his face, he carries it like a trophy.

'Mussels, cockles, pipis . . . two fine snapper fillets. And some oysters,' he says as he unwraps the parcel. 'We'll have the oysters as our entrée, and then I will cook a perfect birthday paella for our main. Are you okay with that?'

She laughs and nods.

'I am perfectly okay with that.'

'A shame we have no champagne, but we do have this!' he says, and takes out two bottles of red wine.

'Finest pinot noir this country can offer.'

He opens the wine and pours two glasses. She doesn't know where the glasses have come from, but they are fine and very thin.

He holds up his glass and they toast. He reaches out his empty hand and pulls her to him. She spills some wine and it runs over her hand. He bends forwards and licks it up. Then he kisses her and she can taste the wine on his tongue.

It is almost dark before the food is ready to eat. They eat slowly, allowing time to stand still.

When they have finished, she goes to fetch the birthday present. He has lit a hurricane lamp and it lights a small sphere around them, leaving the rest of the world in complete darkness.

Carefully, he opens the small package and takes out the CD.

'It won't mean anything in particular to you, that music, but I have a lot of memories connected with it. Good memories,' she says. 'I thought that you might come to like it too. That it might come to mean something to you.'

He looks at her, and in the light of the lamp his eyes are almost black.

'It already does,' he says. 'And when we get back to civilisation, we can listen to it together. You can share your memories with me, while we create new ones.'

They have spread a blanket in front of the tent and they lie close together, her head resting on his chest. The moon is rising, veiled tonight, as if seen *through gauze. The wind has died and all they can hear is the strange, all-permeating sound of invisible cicadas.*

It is much later. He is asleep but she is awake, lying behind him in the tent with her hands on his back.

Even before her fingers touch the spot, inside the fold between his back and his left arm, it is as if they know what they are searching for. As if they have known all along, just been biding their time. Allowing them a little time. Perhaps her eyes have known too, but chosen not to acknowledge what they have seen. Given her another day.

Well before her brain registers, her fingers have already felt the thin scar that runs into his left armpit. A half-moon-shaped scar. So very small, so insignificant. So easily missed.

But her fingers have felt it. There is nothing that she can do to change that. Nothing at all.

She falls headlong into absolute nothingness. It is as if the world has dissolved.

Her hand still rests on his back, but she is no longer there.

She is nowhere, has nowhere to go.

I started when I heard George knock quietly on the door. He stood on the doorstep watching me.

'Sorry, did I frighten you?'

'No,' I said. 'I was just lost in my thoughts.'

'Well, we were wondering where you were,' he said with an embarrassed smile.

'I'm sorry, I was sitting here thinking, and I lost track of time. Give me a couple of minutes to get dressed.'

On my way to the bedroom I called back for him to help himself to a glass of wine.

What is it with this man? I thought to myself when we were in the car on our way to his house. Why does he never ask anything? He must have questions . . .

I couldn't understand why he had said he was a bad cook. He had put together a proper feast. A barbecued butterflied leg of lamb, so tender and tasty that it must have been carefully marinated. How long had he been planning this meal? Baked kumara, salad. And bread that I suspected was home-made. When I praised the food he stood up and began to clear the table, as if he found it difficult to accept the compliment. Ika helped and I watched him as he darted around the kitchen. He seemed right at home here, knew his way around the drawers and cupboards, and the two of them seemed to co-operate almost intuitively.

Did I feel another stab of envy? And if so, why? Which of the two did I envy?

After dinner we sat in the lounge. I looked around. It was a spacious and cosy room, but now I saw it a little differently. I thought I could see that it looked untouched somehow. As if lost in time. There was a grand piano but it was closed. On it stood a portrait of a young woman. I thought she looked beautiful, but I didn't want to make a point of staring at her, and averted my eyes.

But George must have caught my glance because as he sat down he nodded towards the portrait.

'My wife was a pianist,' he said. 'A very talented concert pianist. But she had an accident and broke her wrist. It didn't heal properly, and, well, it was the end of her career. I think I was more devastated than she was. Lidia was . . .' He searched for the word. 'She was a very positive person. Always able to see possibilities where I saw problems. It was her idea to come here. To begin a new, different life.'

He held out a plate of small biscuits and I helped myself.

'And it did turn out differently. Not a different life. Just different. Lidia died in a car accident. I was left here.'

'What made you stay?' I asked, instantly regretting the question.

He sat with his hands gripped between his knees, looking down.

'Where would I have gone?' he said, and lifted his gaze.

I nodded. There was no answer to that question and it lingered between us for a while.

Then George stood and walked over to the piano.

'I have just had it tuned but it will never really be a good piano again. It's a little like it is with people – you can't leave them alone without care for too long. They will never be the same again.'

He removed the portrait and opened the lid. Then he turned and waved to Ika to come and sit on the stool while he returned to the sofa.

Ika played what seemed to me like improvised little pieces. He seemed quite engrossed in the music and one piece followed another seamlessly. I sat back against the cushions, listening. George served coffee. Then he disappeared back into the kitchen and returned with a bottle and two glasses.

'Calvados,' he said, and held up the bottle. 'Would you like some?'

I didn't really know what it was, but at that stage I would have accepted anything just to have the evening stretch out a little longer. So I nodded and George poured.

We sat in comfortable silence listening to the music, until Ika suddenly stood up.

'Finished?' I asked.

He nodded, and turned and disappeared.

After a while he returned and stood in the doorway, at a safe distance from us. He was in his pyjamas, and I noticed they were new. He gave us a vague wave and turned, and we said goodnight to his back.

'I used to go with him to the sleepout,' George said, 'but I soon realised he prefers to be on his own. He takes his torch and disappears out there when he has had enough of my company.'

George gestured for me to follow him over to the window.

We watched Ika run across the back lawn, a small dark figure trailing the beam of a torch. We waited until he had disappeared into his little house and we could see a faint light through the window.

We sat back down on the sofa.

'A drop more?' George asked, and when I nodded he poured us both a little.

We talked about Ika, of course. George expected to hear from CYF the following day. He seemed much more hopeful than I was. Perhaps he knew something I didn't. Also, his relationship with Ika was different from mine. I really didn't know this man at all. I had no idea what he was thinking. He had told me he had become fond of Ika, but what did that mean? How serious and how long-term was his commitment?

We were silent for a moment and I felt as if he might have read my mind. For the first time the silence felt a little uncomfortable.

But I was completely wrong.

'I couldn't help seeing the magazine in your bedroom,' he said suddenly. 'It's you, isn't it? On the cover.'

I looked at him, and the silence lasted an eternity.

Then I nodded.

'I just thought it was such a beautiful picture. I didn't mean to pry.'

I felt my eyes fill with tears and I hoped he wouldn't notice.

'Yes, it's a very beautiful picture,' I said and took a sip from my glass. The alcohol burned my tongue, making my tears plausible, I hoped.

And then the silence was no longer awkward. I felt that George expected nothing further. He sat back, resting against the cushions, contemplating the contents of his glass.

'Time for me to leave, I think,' I said.

'I'll drive you home.'

'I'd rather walk,' I said.

'If you'd like company, I'd be happy to come along.'

I shook my head.

'I need to clear my head, and the walk will do me good,' I said.

We said goodbye on the deck, embraced lightly and allowed our cheeks to touch. Then I turned and entered the dark night. When I looked over my shoulder a little later he was still there, a black silhouette in the doorway.

She sees herself as if from a distance. Her body is still there, just as a moment earlier, with her palms on his back and her cheek pressed against his skin. Everything is as it was a moment earlier.

But nothing will ever be as before. When this night is over, there will be nothing. Absolutely nothing. Ever again.

She can't imagine how she will manage. But she has to leave. Walk away, one step at a time, towards nothing.

Her fingertips run gently over the scar. Though her eyes are closed, she can see it. She buries her nose in his hair and inhales the scent. Allows it to merge with the memory that she has avoided for so long.

All the signs – how is it possible that she has not seen them? Surely at some level she must have realised? His birthday – shouldn't she have known when she heard the date? When she saw his bare back where those small drops of sweat glistened along the spine? Had her eyes not run over the thin line that disappeared into the left armpit? Had she simply refused to see? Been unable to stop herself?

This is what she is thinking, hovering now above the two of them.

She doesn't weep. She lies very still so as not to wake him. All night she lies still, close to him, her arms around him. She closes her eyes and thinks that it could all end right now, like this. Just slowly fade away until they were no longer visible.

Together.

But inexorably the morning arrives. The light seeps through the red canvas and flows over everything inside like thin blood. When she notices him waking, she turns away and closes her eyes. She can hear him move about softly and eventually crawl outside, as if not to disturb her. As soon as he has gone, she turns and lies back down on the warmth that lingers where his body has been.

She stays there till there is no warmth left.

Then she stretches out her hand, opens his backpack and quietly pulls out his passport.

Mikael Daniel Frohman.

Born 12 February 1966.

In Engelbrekt parish, Stockholm, Sweden.

She returns the passport.

From above, where she hovers, she watches herself lying there. She wonders how she will ever be able to get up. How she will get through this day. And all the days following.

She lies still until she has no more thoughts. Just a paralysing, completely unmanageable grief.

Eventually he sticks his head through the opening.

'Tired?'

She nods.

'Yes, and a slight headache. Too much wine last night perhaps,' she says. She listens to her own voice and marvels that it sounds normal.

'Give me a few minutes more, and I will join you.'

And she does manage after all. She sits. Runs her fingers through her hair. Wets her fingertips with saliva and wipes her eyes. Crawls outside.

One step at a time, she thinks. I will take one step at a time.

They drink their coffee and he asks if she would like to have a swim before packing up.

She looks up at the sky, which is perfectly clear but with a grey strip along the horizon, as if a front is approaching.

'Perhaps we should pack up now.' She points to the sky. 'It looks like rain.'

When everything is stowed in the car he grabs her arm and pulls her close.

'What's wrong?'

'I'm just a little sad,' she says.

'But this is just the beginning,' he says. 'I have to drive to Auckland today, but I'll try and change my ticket and stay a little longer, so that we can catch up in Auckland. And make plans. Decide where and when and how we'll be together again. I'll ring you as soon as I get to Auckland.'

She nods and smiles. She can't understand how that is possible. Where does it come from, this thin little smile?

Then he kisses her.

Before she lets him go, she takes his face in her hands. And kisses him once more.

As they drive back to Kawhia it feels as if the landscape behind them is gradually dissolving. She is positive there is nothing left.

Suddenly he brakes and points through the windscreen.

There, high in the pale sky, drifts the graceful formation of godwits. She thinks it looks more contained today. It no longer seems to drift back and forth, but moves with purpose across the sky in a northwesterly direction.

They arrive in Kawhia in the afternoon.

He carries her backpack and puts it in the boot of her car and slams it shut.

They stand there together.

Then, for the briefest moment, she thinks: 'I can't. It's impossible.'

Something gives, and she loses her footing, her composure. She holds out her arms and pulls his body to hers. He holds her tightly, lifts her off the ground and whispers in her ear.

'It's only a day or two.'

And then, the unavoidable.

'I love you, Marion.'

She doesn't weep.

She says: 'I love you, Mikael.'

He gets into his car and rolls down the window. He leans out and calls: 'See you in Auckland!'

She stands and watches him drive away, his hand waving until he disappears around a bend.

She sits in her car until someone honks a horn. She realises she is blocking another parked car, and she starts and drives out of the carpark.

Where will she go?

Where would I go?

That was how George had answered my question.

There are moments in life when we find ourselves at a crossroad that we have completely lost the capacity to evaluate. When all we can manage to do is to drift.

I watched myself driving, on my way to nowhere, and even now I could not understand how I had managed to leave.

When I got home from George's, I went inside and sat down at the kitchen table. It was late, and I still felt affected by the wine and the calvados. I lit a candle and placed it on the table.

Although I could not see much of the room I could feel how clean and tidy it was. It felt soothing. As if my home had become stronger and happier, better set to care for me.

I walked into the bedroom and picked up the magazine, sat back down at the kitchen table and opened it.

There they were, Mikael's pictures. Several pages of them. And a large portrait of him. It must have been taken much earlier, because his hair is short. But it is the same smile. The same grey eyes.

I let my finger trace his forehead.

Eventually she has to stop. It's late afternoon but the rain has not yet arrived. The sky is dark and threatening and the sea below is leaden, with white froth topping the waves. The wind is so strong the gusts rock the car. But she gets out. Stands for a moment looking out over the sea.

She reaches into the pocket of her jeans and pulls out her mobile. Lifts her arm high, and with all the power she can muster she throws it in a high arc towards the sea. She can't see where it lands.

She sinks down to the ground beside the car. Finally, she weeps.

She stays there until the rain arrives. It is a driving, hard rain that whips her skin and pulls at her hair. But she lifts her face to it. Invites it. She staggers to her feet and tears off her jacket. Opens her arms and screams into the wind. She stays there until her voice cracks and she is completely soaked.

Then she lies down in the back seat and goes to sleep.

When she wakes it is still dark but she can sense that it is no longer night. She looks at her watch; it is 4.30. She is stiff and cold. But something has passed.

She is alive.

She stops in Raglan and has breakfast in a small café. A pale sun has risen. She asks around and finds a small bed and breakfast. The young woman who receives her is heavily pregnant. She smiles a pitying smile at the sight of her sodden guest.

'Terrible weather last night,' she says.

It is an impossible effort to think of an answer, so she just takes the key and walks towards the room.

She undresses and stands in the shower, turning up the heat until her skin blushes.

Then she wraps a blanket tightly around herself, lies down and goes to sleep again.

She stays in Raglan for a week, doing nothing at all. Even the most insignificant decision, the slightest act, is a huge effort. Get up. Dress. Have lunch. Go for a walk. Each stage of the day feels insurmountable and requires all her strength.

The nights are emptiness. She sleeps without dreaming. But it is not dreams that she dreads. It is the thoughts that overwhelm her in the grey early morning hours.

23.

Ika was allowed to stay with George for the time being, and our new existence gradually found its shape and form. We alternated cooking dinner, and Ika slept at my house every now and then. We continued working on our project, and George never asked any questions. He might somehow have found out what we were doing, but if so, he never referred to it.

My home was inspected and I went through the entire caregiver evaluation process. It didn't make me any the wiser; I was still unable to assess my chances.

I watched Ika settle in and develop new routines with George. Routines that didn't include me. I tried to look on it as a positive. A sign that Ika was developing socially. I convinced myself that my only concern was that he might become attached to George, while George was viewing it as a temporary arrangement, no different from the others he had accepted.

It was almost three months before we were called to a meeting with Ika's family. I asked George if it always took this long. He didn't know, his own experience was too limited. Some of the cases he had been involved with had been resolved much more quickly, and a few had taken even longer.

We were to meet at a lawyer's office in Hamilton. George offered to drive. The meeting was at midday, so Ika would be at school.

I woke that morning with the memory of my usual dream. I lay with my eyes closed trying to retrieve it before it faded. It was the same dream. We were walking hand in hand though the eerie forest. We reached the cliff and his hand slid out of mine. But when I looked up, there was no railway bridge. And when I turned my eyes to the water it was no longer distant. I slid down into the water. It was warm, the same temperature as my skin and it didn't feel as if I were submerging but as if I were one with it. It glowed around me, as if lit from above. I saw him moving towards me and when we met he stretched out his arms.

We drifted weightless in the golden water with our arms around each other, and I knew it would never end.

I opened my eyes and looked around the room. After we cleaned the house George had helped me repaint. The bedroom walls were a warm white and I had had copies made of Mikael's pictures and framed them. They were not perfect, just scanned from the magazine, but somehow the loss of sharpness seemed a benefit. It was as if the pictures, just like my memories, had developed a skin, become a little blurred at the edges. Somehow they seemed to have slowly merged and become a whole. All the images had become one. They were on the wall across from my bed and they were the first thing my eyes landed on every morning.

190

I had chosen what to wear the evening before. A sleeveless navy blue dress and a grey cardigan. I stood and looked at them hanging on the wardrobe door. It felt as if I were dressing for a trial where I was the defendant. As if I had to make a trustworthy and respectable impression.

I was ready well before the agreed pickup time and I went outside and lay down in the hammock to wait for George. It was a clear autumn day. High skies and a light breeze.

I had turned on the music in the kitchen and suddenly 'Peace Piece' began to play. And I remembered the long time when I had not been able to listen to it. Then time when I allowed myself to listen without responding.

But now the sound of the tranquil touches found its way inside, I was no longer able to – willing to – resist. I was finally ready to receive it. I closed my eyes and I listened with my entire body.

It no longer hurt, it was just beautiful. Peaceful and beautiful.

She drives to Auckland. She has dreaded this trip, but she can't put it off any longer.

'See you in Auckland,' he had said.

And ever since the city has taken on a new dimension. It is no longer the anonymous city that she left. Now it is the city where he is. If he is still there.

She might run into him. It is possible. How would she survive such a meeting? It is inconceivable. Yet there is a part of her that wills it. Her brain doesn't listen to commands; she cannot control her feelings.

But it is her obligation. She must find a way.

It is absolutely essential, whatever the cost.

And she doesn't meet him. Although her eyes sweep over the crowds of people in the street. When she waits at crossings. Sits in cafés. Occasionally she spots a bronzed back. A head of curly blond hair. And everything stops for a second. But it is never him.

She knows that this is as it must be. She has to find a way of living with it. One minute at a time.

She cannot possibly know that there is no need for her to be on her guard. She flies back to London.

She moves into a small rented flat in Hampstead, near the hospital where she works. It is spring, and when she is off work she walks on the Heath, where the spring flowers open and the magnolia blossoms. She is not aware of having any thoughts or plans. Cautiously, she takes one day at a time.

A month. A year.

It doesn't get any easier, but it changes character. It is like accepting a handicap. Rage and grief slowly turn into acceptance, and the struggle for survival begins. Then adjustment. And a kind of life.

She makes good use of her ability to stow away her memories. Put them in their separate boxes and seal them. But the price is high. So much effort is required that there is virtually nothing left for anything else.

It is just as she has come to believe that she has created a kind of bearable existence that everything collapses.

She is doing her usual rounds. Shopping for the usual things. She stops to look in the odd shop window. Then she enters the bookshop. She has nothing in mind; she is just passing time. She is not interested in the magazine section and she has almost passed it when she meets her own gaze.

She stands frozen, her eyes on the image. Then she puts her shopping bags on the floor and with stiff fingers she takes a copy of the magazine from the shelf. She doesn't open it, just keeps looking at the cover. Then she walks to the checkout and pays.

Afterwards, she can't remember how she made it home. But she does remember when she opened the magazine and read the entire article.

She looks at the pictures first. His photographic album Man and the Sea *has won the Pulitzer Prize. But what she sees is not the photos, but the photographer. She looks at the pictures through his eyes, sees what he has seen. Understands exactly what he was wanting to capture.*

Does she deliberately delay reading the article? Flick past the article to the pictures? In the end it suffices to read the headline. The prize has been awarded posthumously.

He never reached Auckland. The article doesn't give the details, of course. Just 'tragically killed in a car accident on his way'. But she thinks she knows. She imagines that his smile didn't even fade.

'See you in Auckland,' he calls, waving through the window. Then there is a bend in the road and she can no longer see him.

She will never see him again.

For the first time she is forced to acknowledge that she has carried that minuscule possibility as a kind of hope. An impossible possibility that she has refused to give up on.

Her carefully constructed existence falls apart. The walls cave in around her, the ground falls away from under her feet.

We were greeted by the lawyer at her office in Hamilton. She was middle-aged, very nicely dressed in a dark two-piece suit, but she had an air of impatience about her. She took us straight into the meeting room and introduced us to the three people who were waiting inside: two representatives from CYF – a woman I had met before and a man who seemed to be her superior – and a woman who looked to be in her mid-thirties. Lola was not there.

The woman was Lola's half-sister, Nina. My heart skipped a beat. For some reason I had not expected a family member.

Coffee had been laid out on a side table and we all served ourselves before sitting down.

The man from CYF opened the meeting.

Every effort had been made to trace Lola, he said. It had been established that she was living up north, but no permanent home had been identified and it had not been possible to find her. Her family no longer had any contact with her.

They had, however, found trustworthy witnesses who could confirm that Lola had abused Ika on several occasions. He had been admitted to hospital twice with broken bones – an arm once and two ribs the second time. Neither had been reported as suspicious and no enquiry had been undertaken.

Ika had undergone an extensive health checkup. His physical health was good, though there were signs of neglect. His teeth, for example, were in bad condition. His mental state and his skills had been tested and the results had confirmed my suspicions that he had a mild form of autism. But the tests had not given any clear indication as to how serious his problems were, or to what extent they could be attributed to his upbringing.

I glanced around the table. The lawyer looked as if she had other pressing matters waiting. She kept checking her watch discreetly. George sat with his hands clasped in his lap and a neutral expression on his face. The woman from CYF made notes in a small notebook – or she may have been doodling. I reflected that in spite of the crucial effect of the outcome of this meeting on Ika, and although he was the main character, he was oddly absent. Not even when he was mentioned by name did it feel as if we were talking about a real live little boy.

When it was George's turn to speak he kept it short. He just confirmed that Ika had settled in well with him, and that he supported my application wholeheartedly.

Then he turned to me.

'Whatever the outcome, I have now become so fond of him that I simply can't imagine not being allowed to play a part in his future.'

He stopped talking and looked a little embarrassed.

I tried to keep my speech factual. I emphasised how well Ika had developed during the time he had lived with me. And I assured them I would facilitate his contacts with his biological family in every way I could.

The man from CYF looked at me and nodded.

Then he invited Nina to speak.

I looked at her, and now I thought I could discern a vague likeness to Lola. It was the eyes more than anything else. But this woman was fairer than Lola, although not as beautiful as I thought Lola must once have been. Nina looked down-to-earth and sensible. A farmer's wife, perhaps, I thought.

I was completely unprepared for her speech.

'Lola is my older half-sister,' she began, 'but I have not seen her for more than twenty years. The last time was when our mother sent me to help Lola with the twins. I was fifteen and Lola twenty-one.'

She paused briefly. She didn't seem uncomfortable or hesitant, and she chose her words carefully. I found myself liking her.

'I never really knew Lola – she left home when she was fifteen. But Mother thought Lola needed help and it was the school holidays. At first I looked forward to it. I have always liked children. But it was awful. I was scared of Lola. The twins were tiny, newborn and underweight. But she hit them. Slapped them here and there if she was the slightest bit irritated. And she left them crying forever. I called Mother and told her, and said I wanted to come home, but I guess Mother thought it sounded even more like Lola needed help. So I stayed a little longer. Until the day she dropped one of them. She said it was an accident but I couldn't help wondering. It didn't feel right. And we didn't go to the hospital until the following day. By then the baby was just lying all limp and breathing very fast. Lola said I mustn't say a word at the hospital. And while we were there, Lola was very different – kind and nice and good with the babies. The little girl had a serious concussion and was kept in hospital. I called Mother again and cried and begged to be allowed to come home. I left the following day. Lola didn't even say goodbye.'

She paused again.

'There is something wrong with Lola. She has never been like other people. At home she lied all the time. About little insignificant things, too. It was as if she wanted to show that she could make people believe anything. She was proud of it, like it was a valuable skill. She was very good-looking, too, and when she smiled and said something, everybody believed her. It's an illness. Of course, sooner or later she gets exposed for what she is and has to move on. Find a new audience. In her sick world there's no room for anybody else. Her relationships have all been short and violent. Her children had awful childhoods. The twins might have done a little better because they were fostered out when they were little, and later adopted. But the other two must have suffered terribly, even though nothing was ever reported. And now they are both dead.'

She took a sip of water.

'What I would like to say is that Lola should never have been allowed to care for a child. I have never met her grandchild, but I would have offered to take him in if I had been able to. I have thought about it carefully, and I simply can't. I have four children and my youngest is handicapped after a brain injury. My husband and I don't think we can give Mika the care he needs and deserves.'

I took a deep breath.

'When I listened to what Marion said I could see how much she seems to care. I'm convinced she really loves this little boy, and I think he would get the very best care in her home.'

She looked at us all around the table.

'It is not my decision of course. But I'd like to state that Mika's family, as represented by me, fully support Marion's appeal. I hope this helps.'

She turned to me.

'And I look forward to staying in touch.'

She smiled at me. As if she assumed that all would go well.

The man from CYF and his colleague ended the meeting, stating that they had made a note of our statements and that a decision would likely be made within a couple of days. Then we all said our goodbyes.

I would have liked to talk to Nina but she had to rush off – her husband was waiting outside. She gave me a quick hug and a peck on the cheek.

'What do you think?' I asked when we were in the car on our way home.

George turned and looked at me.

'It's obvious, isn't it?' he said. 'After Nina's endorsement I can't imagine it won't go your way.'

After a little while he threw me another quick glance.

'And I meant every word I said.'

24.

The call came the following Friday. Such a brief conversation, yet my life was completely changed in an instant. Or perhaps my life had just begun.

I sank down on a chair after I had put the phone down.

It felt strange, the laughter. Hesitant and frail, like the first thin trickle in a dried-out riverbed. But it gained momentum, till it burst out of me. I ran out onto the deck, lifted my arms to the sky. Danced like a madwoman. Then I started to run.

I arrived completely out of breath. I found George in a sunchair at the back of his house, reading the paper.

He slowly stood up as he spotted me. I ran up to him and threw my arms around his neck.

It took a moment before he responded. It seemed as if he hesitated for a second or two, to give me an opportunity to change my mind. To make sure it wasn't just a rash impulse. Then I felt how he embraced me, hard, lifted me off the ground and twirled around on the grass with me in his arms.

'It's done!' I said when he put me down and I had regained my breath. 'Ika is staying.'

Then I kissed him.

25.

I walked along the beach. There were a couple of hours until it was time to collect Ika from school. We had agreed to go together – George would pick me up.

There was a nip in the air and the sand was cool under my feet. I remembered the time Ika and I had talked about place. This place and other places, and he had asked me if I was always going to stay here. Then, my answer had come out spontaneously and I hadn't hesitated for even a second. I had thought that I would stay here until my life was over.

Since I came to live here I had never been further than Auckland. There had been days, sometimes weeks, when I hadn't left this beach at all.

Now, when I looked around I suddenly saw that my well-known

setting was undergoing a subtle change. Not in how it looked, but in how it felt. It felt as if it was retreating. I let my eyes wander over the familiar sand dunes, where earlier I had thought that I knew every line, every shadow, and they looked different. It felt as if I was about to be delivered out of the environment that had protected me for so long.

I had not thought any further ahead than this day. Now that it had arrived, I realised I would have to make plans. Even if they did not include any major changes, my life would never be as before. I am not sure if it had quite dawned on me before that I now had to consider a future.

I had lived for so long without a future, and with a locked-away past. Every day had been a matter of survival, one day at a time. I had never looked back, and never forwards, but lived in some kind of eternal present.

I wandered down to the edge of the water. The odd wave reached me, and the cold water swept over my feet. I looked out to sea. I wondered if perhaps I had finally gained that sense of wholeness that I had always associated with the sea. I wondered whether I now had the capacity to live a life that contained a past as well as a future.

Whatever lay in store.

It is instinct that drives her. She is fighting for her life. For some measure of life. Or perhaps it is not life she is seeking. Perhaps it is a place to die.

So she leaves and travels again to the other side of the earth. It is a pilgrimage, perhaps, and a temple that she is hoping to find.

A place where one day she will be able to open her memories.

If I am not able to live here, and wait for that day, then I can die here, she thinks.

She takes one day at a time.

Walks along her lonely beach. Meandering, tentative walks, searching for something she never finds.

But time passes. And she lives a sort of life in the cocoon of loneliness she has woven around herself.

Somehow, and for some reason, she survives. Creates an existence that isn't life, but a vague resemblance.

Sometimes she marvels at the fact that she is still here, that she is still alive.

And although she knows why she has chosen this place, she doesn't allow herself even the slightest recollection of that which has brought her here, doesn't even brush against it.

But it has happened that she has taken the car and driven to Kawhia. There, she has not even left the car, just parked where she saw him drive away. She sits there and she doesn't understand why.

But she never returns to the place where they camped.

26.

'I think this calls for a proper celebration,' George said after dinner that Friday.

Ika nodded, and he looked like a serious grown-up man. It was moving to see how he had already acquired several of George's mannerisms.

I laughed this strange, recently recovered laughter that still startled me.

'But we already have,' I said, and pointed to what remained of our meal. 'A superb dinner.'

I lifted my wine glass and proposed a toast.

'Sometimes we are given exactly what we need. Those precise people that you need the most come stumbling into your life. Sometimes you don't notice, and this is very sad. Sometimes you lose them again. This is sad too, but not as sad. Because what you have once had together, you have forever. Dear Ika, I am so very happy I found you lying by my feet that day. And I am so very grateful that you have stayed in my life. Now we have each other forever, whatever happens.'

Ika raised his glass and glanced briefly in my direction.

'And you, George,' I said, and turned to him. 'I am so happy that I finally took notice of you. And I am sorry it took so long. And so very grateful that you were still around when I lifted my eyes.'

And so we toasted.

George cleared his throat.

'I am not sure that it is a great idea,' he said, 'but I have something different in mind. Something special.'

Ika looked at George, and his gaze fixed on him properly.

'I think we should make an excursion,' George said.

'Where?' Ika and I said with one voice.

George smiled his secretive little smile.

'I thought it should be a surprise. Does tomorrow suit?'

We nodded and I asked if there was anything I could bring.

George shook his head.

'Nothing at all,' he said.

We helped clear the table and then we said goodnight.

George put his hand lightly on my shoulder, and again I felt as if he was waiting for my reaction. I put my hand on top of his and then I took a step closer and put my cheek against his.

'Thank you,' I said. 'For everything.'

He put his arms around me and pulled me close. Then abruptly he let go and took my hand instead.

'Come here,' he said to Ika.

To my utter surprise, Ika stepped forwards. George put his hand on Ika's head and gently brought him closer. For a moment we stood like that, forming a small unity.

Then Ika and I wandered home.

I turned to wave one last time, but George had turned off the light in the hall and I couldn't be sure whether he was still there on his deck.

I thought so, though, and Ika and I both waved.

It was late when we got home, but it was Friday so it didn't matter. We sat on the deck for a while, Ika in his usual spot in the hammock and I on the top step.

Suddenly I heard his voice from the hammock.

'Now we're home,' he said.

I nodded to myself.

'Yes, now we're home.'

27.

George arrived the following morning as agreed. It was sunny and clear and we had the road to ourselves. We drove north, along the sea. I tried to guess where we were heading. To Raglan? But when we reached Raglan we turned east. Eventually I gave up trying to guess and leaned back in my seat to enjoy the journey.

George had brought coffee in a thermos and juice for Ika and a muffin each, and we made a short stop on the roadside and ate and drank. Ika didn't seem any more curious than I was, and he asked no questions.

Finally we left the main road. Cows grazed peacefully on either side of the narrow road and we travelled slowly.

'A helicopter!' Ika called out.

I looked at George and his smile was wider than ever.

We were going to have a helicopter ride.

And George was the pilot.

I stared at him.

'You have many secret skills,' I said.

He just smiled.

Ika sat beside George and I sat in the back seat. It was my first helicopter ride. I told myself it was no different from putting our lives in George's hands when we travelled in his car. Somehow it didn't quite feel the same though.

But as soon as we gained height and the landscape spread out below us, I forgot my objections and my anxiety dissolved.

It was stunningly beautiful.

I was completely entranced, struck dumb. But George and Ika were communicating with their hands, pointing this way and that. We flew in a wide sweep towards the coast. It took me a while to realise where we were heading.

We flew in over my beach and I could make out my house.

But my house was not our goal.

It was our project.

I could see that Ika had realised this too.

For the first time I could see it as he had always been able to see it.

We descended and it expanded, like a painting under our feet.

Absolutely perfect.

Two trails – waves, I imagined – that belonged together but were distinctly separate at the same time. The impression was so perfect that I almost saw them move, softly intertwining in a constant graceful interplay.

George made several sweeps at different altitudes. It was breath-taking from all perspectives.

I tapped Ika on the shoulder and bent forwards. He turned so that I could see his profile. He was smiling.

We made one last turn and I thought we were heading back, but George continued south.

We flew in over Kawhia and the harbour.

Out towards the sea.

Then we continued in a wide semicircular movement across the inlet.

There it was, the peninsula, framed by the dark blue-green sea. The place I had avoided even thinking about. The place I had convinced myself had dissolved in the dust behind the car when we left.

I could see it, embrace it as a part of a past that I wanted to retain, as well as a part of a future I was now welcoming.

We flew higher, and below us the individual features of the landscape gradually merged.

Everything merged and became a whole.

Acknowledgements

At the best of times, writing a novel is a solitary occupation. The work stretches over a long period of time, and often feels like wandering alone in a landscape that is being created as it is explored – a landscape with no certain pathways, no landmarks, alien and tempting at the same time.

2010 was not the best of times for me and without the support from family and friends, I might have been forever lost in my landscape and this book would not have been written. I wish to thank all of you who kept believing in what I was trying to do, showed me the way and made me believe, too. I am sure you know who you are.

I also wish to thank Lorraine Hoult, who tirelessly talked to me about the work of those who look out for the smallest and most vulnerable in our society. With patience and respect she answered all my questions, however simple and trivial, and in the process she changed the way I view the work of Child, Youth and Family, CYF, forever. In a sense, what I learned opened my eyes and came to change the way I view our entire society.

Finally, my sincere gratitude to my editor, Rachel Scott, who has again miraculously transformed my manuscript, while making me believe it was my own doing.

Linda Olsson
Auckland, October 2011

A PENGUIN READERS GUIDE TO

THE MEMORY OF LOVE

Linda Olsson

An Introduction to
The Memory of Love

The Memory of Love tells a story of extraordinary emotional depth and power. Marion, a retired surgeon, long divorced, lives on a remote beach in New Zealand. She looks back over the course of her life, trying to make sense of who she was, who she has become, and all the seemingly disparate story lines that have brought her to where she is. She wants urgently to feel whole again after years of tragedy, heartbreak, and numbness.

Into her solitary life comes an unusual boy, Ika, who Marion discovers lying facedown on the beach. Quiet, mysterious, musically gifted, and probably suffering from some degree of autism, Ika profoundly affects Marion. He visits her every Thursday, and for reasons she doesn't clearly understand, she feels "an inexplicable sense of anticipation. As if the opening of doors and tearing away of layers was a positive thing" (p. 9). They begin to work together on a kind of natural art project in a cove, and Marion cooks for him and teaches him piano. As the time passes, a deep and unspoken affinity and affection develops between them.

3

One week, when Ika inexplicably doesn't show up for their usual Thursday lunch, Marion senses something has happened. She searches desperately and finds him on the beach again, this time nearly drowned, with bruises all over his body. Suddenly, her involvement in Ika's life becomes much more complicated. It's clear that Ika's home life is not safe and Marion must decide how to help him.

As the story unfolds, flashbacks from Marion's past reveal a life filled with trauma, fear, and loneliness: the wrenching separation from her beloved grandfather when her mother—a beautiful, ambitious, emotionally distant actress—takes her to live in Stockholm; the violent deaths of her mother and stepfather; and another painful separation, this time from her baby brother, when she is forced to live with her uncle after her parents die. The events of her life have led Marion to shut down emotionally in order to survive. She wills herself to erase the past, to become a different person with a new name, *Marion*, instead of her given name of *Marianne*.

But the past has an uncanny way of showing up again, however hard Marion has tried to keep it at bay. Her relationship with Ika serves as an invitation both to reconnect with her painful history and to create a new kind of life, one that would integrate all that she's been through and allow her to move forward with a sense of wholeness.

Lyrical, unflinchingly honest, and emotionally complex, *The Memory of Love* explores the limits of what the human heart can endure—and the grace that waits inside the most painful losses.

About the Author

Linda Olsson was born in Stockholm, Sweden. In 2003, she won the *Sunday Star-Times* (New Zealand) Short Story Competition. Olsson lived in Kenya, Singapore, Britain, and Japan before settling in Auckland, New Zealand. She now divides her time between Sweden and New Zealand. She is the author of two previous novels, *Astrid & Veronika* and *Sonata for Miriam*, both international bestsellers.

A Conversation with Linda Olsson

What drew you to write this particular story? Is there much overlap between your own experience and the characters or situations described in the book?

For me, the writing always begins with a person, a character. Just like with meetings in real life, I don't know much about my characters initially. In a sense, it feels like the characters take me by the hand and invite me to accompany them on the journey that becomes the novel. With *The Memory of Love*, Marianne/Marion was more elusive than my previous characters have been. I saw her clearly, and I knew that her story contained the loss of a brother, but her place and time remained obscure for quite a while. I tried different settings, but only when it finally became clear to me that she belonged in New Zealand in a similar way to how I do myself, everything fell into place. But her story is not mine, and I have not had her experiences. It is often said that authors bring something of themselves to all their characters and I think that, in this case, my character's emotions felt familiar. I found it easy, and perhaps even to a degree therapeutic, to write her story.

You dedicate the book to your mother, and mother-child relationships are central in the novel. Could you talk about your relationship with your mother and the importance of mothering in The Memory of Love?

I have dedicated this book to my mother, but not in her capacity as my mother. It was the image of the little girl that she once was, and her relationship with her brother, that filled my mind as I wrote. Although the stories are different, my mother's traumatic childhood and her dependency on her brother inspired the creation of Marianne/Marion.

Many readers have pointed out that my books have no good mothers. The mothers in my novels are absent, dead, neglectful, or simply unable to nurture and love their children. I think there is a reason for the special place that the idea of maternal love holds—in real life, and symbolically in all cultures and all times. I do believe that it is essential in order for a child to grow into a caring, confident adult who is able to give love. It would be nice to think that motherly love flows instinctively when a child is born. Sadly, this is not so. A childhood without motherly love leaves the child without the sense of self-worth that is required in order to be able to love. In a sense such children will remain children all their lives. When Marianne/Marion meets the little boy Ika, I think they both find something in the other to fill the void that a lost mother has left behind. The little boy quietly seeks the woman's company, and there is a scene in the book where Marianne/Marion asks herself who is rescuing whom, who has the greatest need of the other. For me, it's a comforting thought that we are free to search for the people to guide and help us. The replacements for the mothers we never had. Looking back on my own life, I think I have done so.

You worked in finance before becoming a full-time writer. Did the shift to writing fiction feel like a radical change for you or the fulfillment of something that was waiting to come forth all along?

At the time, when the great shifts in my life have taken place, I have hardly noticed. It is only in hindsight that I have been able to see a kind of pattern. Even a plan, perhaps, though I am not sure it was entirely my own. I studied law and finance in a search for security, I think. And perhaps some kind of recognition. Proving to myself and to others that I could do it. I was the first member of my family to be given the opportunity to pursue a university degree, and it did feel like a gift as well as a responsibility. I think that with a different background I might have felt freer to pursue my genuine interests, and I would probably have ended up in art school. Instead, I graduated with a degree in law and finance. When my first novel was published in Sweden, a former colleague sent me a letter congratulating me, saying that he was not in the least surprised, as my writing had always been "very creative." And my old teacher told me at the launch party that he had always thought I would be working with words. "I didn't think you would be a novelist, but perhaps a journalist," he said. And now, looking back, I think that my education gave me what I set out to gain: a sense of security. Not so much financial security, though I have been fortunate in this respect, too, but more a belief in myself. A level of self-worth that the women in my family have sadly gone without.

Marion feels like an outsider in the village. Is this a feeling that you've identified with in your life or that has played into your journey as a writer?

I did find it easy to relate to Marion's sense of distance. She is an outsider in the community where she lives. She is also a very lonely person, which is not always the same thing. Like Marion, I have ended up living in a part of the world far removed from where I grew up. And like her, I have come to realize that however much I feel just like the locals, they don't see me like one of them. Being an outsider, an immigrant, is not necessarily a negative thing. It can give you the opportunity to change your life, to be what you want to be. In the novel, Marion says, "They called me 'the artist'. And they called me 'the doctor'. Or just 'her' or 'that foreign woman'. Making it clear that somehow I was not one of them. To them I had no name, just a designation." I suspect that people I know in New Zealand would refer to me as "that Swedish woman," which immediately puts me in a category of my own. But when I return to Sweden, where people refer to me in the same way they would any fellow Swede, I still often sense a distance, even in regard to my friends. So much of my life has no connection with Sweden. And with my family, it is not just a case of geographical separation, but also an educational and social distance. Thinking about my books, I realize that many of my characters are outsiders, by choice or by circumstances beyond their control. Like me, they are people who have a fluid relationship with place, and they seek their security in close relationships to human beings.

Why did you choose Adrienne Rich's poem "From a Survivor" as an epigraph for The Memory of Love? *Has she been an important writer for you?*

Yes, I have loved and admired her poetry since I studied literature when I first came to New Zealand. The wonderful quality of the best poetry is its ability to relate to the reader in a very personal way, making you feel that the words have been written for you exclusively.

The Memory of Love *is on some essential level about the loss of—and longing for—family. Could you talk about the differences between the families we are born with and the families we create as adults, like the one that Marion creates with Ika and George?*

I recently read this quote by the Roman philosopher Seneca, "We are in the habit of saying that it was not in our power to choose the parents who were allotted to us, that they were given to us by chance. But we can choose whose children we would like to be." I found it immensely comforting. In Swedish there is a term called "Dandelion Children." They are children who have somehow managed to grow like little weeds, without nourishment or sunshine, pushing through minute cracks in the road surface or wherever they have found a glimpse of air and light. They are children who seem to own an irrepressible will to live. I think the loss of a "real" family, for whatever reason, will leave a child with a scar. But for those who have been rejected or abandoned such scars take longer to heal, or may never heal at all. All my life I have longed for a big family, and I consider my divorce the greatest sorrow of my adult life. However, when it happened, my children were adults and they have the benefit of all their family members on both sides.

Marion is driven to find a sense of wholeness and continuity with her past, the very painful experiences she's lived through and tried to keep from being overwhelmed by. Why is it so important for us to make sense of our personal histories?

The ability to reconcile all aspects of our lives, to embrace our entire life history is required in order to make us whole human beings. In order to love and forgive others, we need to love and forgive ourselves. Everything begins with ourselves. It's like the safety instructions that we get on airplanes: put on your own oxygen mask before attending to others. I do think that it is crippling to live with aspects of your life locked inside. This doesn't mean that we need to discuss them openly. We just need to acknowledge them and accept them.

Is there a lively literary culture in New Zealand and Sweden? How do you feel about living in two different countries?

Frustrated! I am constantly struggling to catch up. Not just with the literature—which is very lively in both countries—but with all aspects of life. The last few years, it has felt as if I am trying to live twelve months in every six-month period as I move from one country to the other. Two of my three sons live in New Zealand, one in Sweden. After my divorce, when I was free to make my own decision about my living conditions, I thought I would move back to Europe, possibly back to Sweden. However, after almost three years I am still living this double life, and I have come to think that perhaps this is meant to be.

What other Swedish or New Zealand writers would you recommend to your readers?

Where to start?

New Zealand literature is largely unknown outside New Zealand. It is difficult to understand why this is so, as there is a wealth of wonderful New Zealand authors, and they all write in English. Apart from a handful of authors like Katherine Mansfield and Janet Frame, very few are known internationally. It might be due to the geographical isolation, and perhaps also a lack of cultural confidence. New Zealand is a young country and its literature has no iconic epic novel, but many authors excel in a smaller format. There are many wonderful poets and writers of short stories. Frank Sargeson, Owen Marshall, and Patricia Grace are some of my favorites. Another favorite is Maurice Gee and I hope that his novels will soon reach a larger audience. Among the younger writers I like Lloyd Jones and Paula Morris, to mention a few.

Apart from crime literature, not much Swedish literature reaches a wider international audience. Yet there are many fine authors. I return again and again to the classics: August Strindberg and Hjalmar Söderberg, for example. I never quite catch up with the newcomers, but I did read Tomas Bannerhed's first novel *Korparna* (*The Crows*) which won the finest Swedish literary award, the August Prize, in 2011. It is a truly wonderful novel, very Swedish, set in the countryside in the southeast of the country, but also, like all good literature a brilliant illustration of fundamental existential issues.

What are you working on now?

I have started on a new novel. This time the time and the place are absolutely clear, but the direction is still a little unclear. I am taking small steps, and I walk slowly. This time, it will be a very Swedish novel, firmly set in the part of Stockholm where the Swedish part of me feels at home, but there is a reason for the many divergences that the plot will make, in place and in time. I am also working on another major project together with a much younger colleague. This is firmly set in New Zealand, but just like in my own novel, this plot has important international aspects. So, it looks like I will continue my double life for the foreseeable future.

Questions for Discussion

1. What is the particular appeal of reading this kind of emotionally rich and complex novel? Does witnessing Marion's struggle to make sense of her life help you to make sense of your own?

2. How is little Marianne affected by being taken from her grandfather to live with her mother and Hans in Stockholm? What coping strategies does she develop to manage her loneliness, fear, and confusion?

3. What is the effect of the narrative moving back and forth between Marion's past and present? What are some of the most surprising and traumatic moments in her personal history? Why would Olsson choose to reveal these moments gradually rather than all at once?

4. Late in the novel, Marion tries to look at her relationship with Ika objectively and asks herself, "Had I used him? Was he simply a tool for me to give my soul peace? Redeem myself? Could I ever isolate my feelings for Ika from my past? See him as he was, see his true needs?" (p. 171). In what ways might Marion's personal history have colored her relationship with Ika? Is she using him to fulfill her own needs or is she motivated more by compassion than selfishness?

5. In what ways does her relationship with Ika change Marion? Why would a mostly silent, slightly autistic nine-year-old boy lead to such major transformations in her? In what ways does he serve as a doorway into her buried past?

6. What is the significance of Marion first finding Ika lying on the beach? Does it remind her of earlier events in her life?

7. Marion, Ika, and George have all suffered major losses. Marion has lost her parents, her brother, and her grandfather, as well as her husband through divorce. Ika's mother died soon after giving birth to him, and he never knew his father. George has lost his wife. "My home died with my wife," he says (p. 156). In what ways might these losses have prepared them to create a new family, and a new home, with each other? Is there any way these terribly painful experiences can be seen as gifts?

8. Why does Marion feel compelled to make sense of her life, her history? Why is it so important to put the events of her life in some kind of order, to see it "as a whole"? (p. 9). How does she find that wholeness and accept her past by the end of the book?

9. Why does Olsson end the novel with George taking Marion and Ika on a helicopter flight over the project Marion and Ika have been working on? What is the significance of this heightened perspective and of Marion and Ika being able to see their project in its entirety rather than just its individual parts?

To access Penguin Readers Guides online,
visit the Penguin Group (USA) Web site at www.penguin.com.

AVAILABLE FROM PENGUIN

Sonata for Miriam

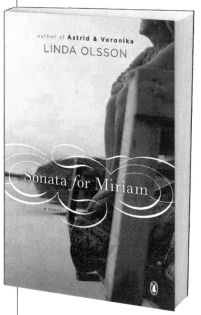

Linda Olsson charts the terrain of human relationships in a novel that explores the significant impact of history on individual lives. In *Sonata for Miriam*, two events occur that will change composer Adam Anker's life forever. Embarking on a journey that ranges from New Zealand to Poland and then Sweden, Anker uncovers his parents' true fate during World War II and finally faces the consequences of an impossible choice he was forced to make twenty years before.

PENGUIN
BOOKS